D0949549

LAURA INGALLS WILDER'S
LOST LITTLE HOUSE YEARS

Old Town in the Green Groves

THE LITTLE HOUSE BOOKS
By Laura Ingalls Wilder

———————

LAURA INGALLS WILDER'S
LOST LITTLE HOUSE YEARS

Old Town in the Green Groves

BY CYNTHIA RYLANT

ILLUSTRATED BY JIM LaMARCHE

HarperCollins*Publishers*

Having researched dozens of sources for this book, the author wishes
to acknowledge in particular the helpfulness of these works:

Growing Up With the Country: Childhood on the Far-Western Frontier, by Elliott West
The Laura Ingalls Wilder Family Series, by William Anderson

Parts of this novel were inspired by Laura Ingalls Wilder's unpublished
manuscript *Pioneer Girl* © 1978 Little House Heritage Trust

HarperCollins®, ♣®, and Little House® are trademarks of
HarperCollins Publishers, Inc.

Old Town in the Green Groves
Text copyright © 2002 by Cynthia Rylant
Illustrations copyright © 2002 by Jim LaMarche
Printed in the United States of America. For information address
HarperCollins Children's Books, a division of HarperCollins Publishers,
1350 Avenue of the Americas, New York, NY 10019.
www.harperchildrens.com

Library of Congress Cataloging-in-Publication Data
Rylant, Cynthia.
   Old town in the green groves : Laura Ingalls Wilder's lost little house years / by Cynthia
Rylant ; illustrated by Jim LaMarche.
   "A little house book."
   Summary: After grasshoppers ruin the crops, eight-year-old Laura Ingalls and her family
leave Plum Creek and move to Burr Oak, Iowa, where they experience life in a small town
and help manage a hotel.
   ISBN 0-06-029561-9 — ISBN 0-06-029562- (lib. bdg.)
   1. Wilder, Laura Ingalls, 1867–1957—Childhood and youth—Juvenile fiction.   [1. Wilder,
Laura Ingalls, 1867–1957—Childhood and youth—Fiction.   2. City and town life—Iowa—
Fiction.   3. Frontier and pioneer life—Minnesota—Fiction.   4. Family life—Fiction.
5. Hotels, motels, etc.—Fiction.   6. Burr Oak, (Iowa)—Fiction.   7. Minnesota—Fiction.]
I. LaMarche, Jim, ill.   II. Title.
PZ7.R982 Ol   2002   2001024594
[Fic]—dc21   CIP
                                                                                    AC

1   2   3   4   5   6   7   8   9   10

First Edition

FOREWORD

This is a story based on the life of Laura Ingalls Wilder between the winter of 1875 and the fall of 1877. Laura is eight years old when this story begins.

When she grew up and wrote the Little House books about her childhood, Laura Ingalls Wilder did not write about this period of time in her life. In the series, the Ingalls family moves directly from the banks of Plum Creek (the fourth book) to the shores of Silver Lake (the fifth). But in real life, in between these times, Laura actually lived with her family in a small town in Iowa called Burr Oak.

In her many years as a writer, Laura Ingalls Wilder penned only a dozen pages about this part of her life, and those pages were never published.

Still, she always remembered Burr Oak as "a lovely place," and many good things happened to her there. I was asked to write about this time of her life.

Relying on Mrs. Wilder's few written memories and on the wonderful spirit that lives in all of her books, I have crafted this "lost" story.

It is for Laura.

C.R.

CONTENTS

LAURA INGALLS WILDER'S
LOST LITTLE HOUSE YEARS

Old Town in the Green Groves

A Rented House

It was wintertime on the prairie, and things were changing all around Laura as she walked to school each morning. The wide prairie skies were no longer softly blue and filled with the voices of bobolinks and meadowlarks and sparrows. Now gray clouds had settled low over the land, and they promised a time of snow and cold and the hungry call of blackbirds in the brown, empty fields. Laura loved the winter for its stillness and its gray-white beauty. But she also knew it could be cruel. She had lived on the prairie long enough to learn that.

Laura was not so worried about what surprises winter might bring this year, for Pa had moved the whole family from their farm on Plum Creek to a snug little rented house behind the church in Walnut Grove. Walnut Grove was a newly settled town on the Minnesota prairie, and it was the safest place to be when the hard blizzards blew in and there was nothing to do but shiver and shake and wait until the storm gave back the land. On Plum Creek blizzards had been hard. Pa had nearly died in one. And some neighbors had died from being lost in the snow.

But in a little house in town the Ingalls family would be safer and happier. Pa wouldn't get lost in a blinding white storm as he drove the wagon home from town. He was already in town. Ma wouldn't worry so and watch the northwest sky for a low, black line of cloud. And Laura and Mary and Carrie would be more cheerful because they could go to school every day instead of staying in their lonely farmhouse all winter, restless and waiting for spring.

Laura liked school, and she was happy to

walk there with her sisters each day. Laura had not thought that she would like school, when she was littler. She hadn't wanted to be away from the warm company of Ma all day. She hadn't wanted to miss Jack, the dear brindle bulldog she loved so well. And most of all, she didn't want to miss Pa and his happy blue eyes and his good cheer and his stories.

But Laura liked school now. She liked it more every day.

"I like school," she said to Mary and Carrie as they made their way along the crisp dirt road leading to the schoolhouse. The sky was still not quite light, and Laura held little Carrie's hand for safety. Carrie was six years old now, but she was still the baby of the family.

"I love school," said Mary, adjusting her shawl against the chilly wind. "I could live there if I didn't love home more."

Laura smiled. Mary had always been the best one at learning. Mary had always been the best at everything. She was kindest. She was the most patient. She minded Ma better. And she wasn't a tomboy, like Laura was sometimes.

Laura knew that she could never be as good as Mary, and she was glad that Ma and Pa had at least one good girl they could be proud of.

"I like singing the letters," said Carrie. "And tag."

Laura smiled and squeezed Carrie's hand. Carrie was a good girl, too.

When the road ended, the girls followed the narrow path leading up to the little white schoolhouse sitting alone on the prairie. Laura could see Frank Carr carrying in the water bucket for Miss Beadle and James Harris toting a load of logs for the fire. Miss Beadle had arrived early and already started up a crackling fire in the potbellied stove and warmed up the frosty-cold classroom. But the cold prairie wind would blow all day long, and all day long the fire would want feeding.

"Good morning, Laura!" said Rebekah when the girls stepped through the schoolhouse door and into the cloakroom to take off their wraps.

"Good morning, Rebekah!" answered Laura. Rebekah was one of Laura's favorite friends. She always had a nice word for everybody and she loved to run, just like Laura.

When everyone had hung their wraps on nails and put their tin lunch pails on the cloak-room bench, it was time to go in and say good morning to Miss Beadle. Then school would begin.

Laura thought Miss Beadle was a fine teacher. She always looked so nice, in her pretty white bodice and her long black skirt and her dark hair pulled back and held with a comb. Miss Beadle always opened the school day with a prayer and a song. This morning the song was "Wait for the Wagon." Laura smiled as she sang, "Wait for the wagon and we'll all take a ride!" She was thinking of Pa and how much he loved taking a wagon west. Laura loved it too. She could go west every day, her whole life long.

At the end of the school day, in a softly falling snow and a steady wind, Laura and her sisters walked back to their home in town. When they passed Oleson's General Store, Laura could see Nellie, Mr. Oleson's spoiled daughter, through the window. Laura imagined Nellie standing in front of one of the big store barrels, cramming her mouth full of candy until bedtime. Then Laura decided not to think about Nellie at all. She walked on toward the small church with the belfry on top. Behind the church there was home.

Soon Laura and her sisters opened the front door of their little rented house and stepped inside. Ma had a pot of beans on the stove, cooking with a side of pork, and the warm house smelled wonderful. Ma had always made every place they had ever lived wonderful. She called it making a place "homelike." And here, in this small house that wasn't even their own, she had done all the special things that made it home. She had covered the kitchen table with the pretty red-checked tablecloth and on it had put their precious family books: the Bible, *Wonders of the Animal World*, and the novel *Millbank*, which Ma liked to read aloud to Pa.

She had hung her crisp white curtains with calico trim on the windows. She had set the faithful rocker by the stove. She had hung up the beautiful wooden bracket Pa had made and on it set the precious china shepherdess she had carried from place to place for years.

Warm quilts covered the beds, feather pillows topped those, and soft lantern light lit everything with a gentle yellow glow.

Ma was sewing up a nightcap for Carrie when the girls arrived. Ma looked especially happy, and as she helped the girls off with their wraps, she asked them about school and the things they had learned. Ma used to be a schoolteacher herself, and she valued a good education, for she considered it "the great equalizer."

Laura, Mary, and Carrie all crowded near the stove to warm their fingers and eat bread with molasses as they told their school stories. Carrie sang a little song she had learned about a frog. Mary recited a verse of poetry by John Keats perfectly. And Laura told of how Donald had pulled her braid to slow her down as they were racing back inside from recess.

"Laura!" cautioned Ma. "You mustn't be too rambunctious. You are nearly nine years old now, and you must behave with the manners of a young lady."

"Yes, Ma," Laura said. Laura knew that Ma was right. But, oh, how she would miss being rambunctious!

A BUNDLE OF SURPRISE

The next day, when Laura and her sisters came home from school, cold and rosy-cheeked, they found Jack sitting beside the front door looking worried. It was easy to know when Jack was worried. His brow furrowed and his round dark eyes opened rounder, and when he wagged his tail, it wasn't a joyous nonstop wagging. It was a wag. Just one. Jack looked at the girls and wagged once.

Full of sudden fear, Laura petted Jack and followed Mary and Carrie into the house. Something had to be wrong.

Inside, the girls were surprised to find their neighbor Mrs. Taylor in the kitchen. She had a pot of water boiling on the big black stove and was sorting through a small bundle of cloths on the kitchen table.

"Good afternoon, girls!" she said cheerily. Laura knew right away that nothing could really be wrong. Mrs. Taylor sounded too happy. But where was Ma? And where was Pa? His wet overshoes were drying behind the stove.

"Where's Ma?" Mary asked. "Is Pa here?" Laura felt shy, finding someone else besides Ma in charge of their kitchen.

"Right here!" Pa called out, as the bedroom door opened and he stepped into the room. "How are all my girls? Did you shine in school today?"

The girls couldn't answer in their confusion. Here was Pa, but where was Ma?

"Where's Ma?" asked Carrie.

"Ma is resting," said Pa.

"Is she sick?" Laura asked anxiously.

"No, flutterbudget, Ma's fine," said Pa.

"Let's pull off these wraps and get you girls all washed and combed, and then Ma will show you her surprise."

"Surprise?" asked Carrie. "Dolls?"

Pa laughed his bright hearty laugh.

"Not dolls, Carrie," he answered. "But that was a mighty good guess!"

Laura and her sisters hung their shawls and coats and mittens on pegs by the kitchen door and pulled off their cold shoes and set them on a box near the stove. They washed up in a basin of warm water Mrs. Taylor poured for them and smoothed their hair and their dresses. Carrie kept talking about dolls, but slowly Laura was beginning to think she might know what Ma's surprise was. Carrie couldn't guess it, because Carrie was the baby of the family. But Laura and Mary were old enough to remember some things, and small smiles began to bloom on their faces.

Laura looked at Pa. She tried to hide her smile but had trouble holding it back.

"I think I know what the surprise is, Pa," she said solemnly.

"You do, half-pint?" Pa asked with a twinkle. "Well, don't go and spoil it for your little sister. She's working her darnedest to figure things out!"

Pa bent over and took Carrie's hand. He looked into her pretty brown eyes with his own clear blue ones.

"Ready, apple pie?" he asked. "For Ma's surprise?" Carrie nodded her head.

The girls left Mrs. Taylor making tea at the stove, and they followed Pa into the bedroom.

Ma was lying in bed with the feather pillows bunched up behind her and warm quilts over her and a sweet, almost tearful smile on her face. And in her arms, wrapped in warm wool and flannels and sleeping the sleep of angels, was a tiny, tiny baby.

Carrie gasped. "A baby!" she squealed.

"It's a real doll this time," said Pa, lifting her up in his arms.

Laura edged nearer the bed with Mary.

"You have a brother, my dear girls," Ma said softly. "He is named for your father, Charles Frederick."

A *boy*! thought Laura. A little *boy*!

"I'm so glad he's a boy, Ma," said Laura. "We've got enough girls."

The girls took turns kissing the baby's warm pink head and looking carefully at his tiny face all peaceful and calm. They watched him take his small baby breaths. He was beautiful.

"He is so pretty, Ma," said Mary.

"Yes he is, dear," Ma said. "And one day he will be handsome and brave like your father."

Mary smiled. Pa smiled back.

"Well, brave anyhow!" he laughed. "Now, let's get you girls some warm tea, and we'll let Ma and your little brother sleep. Caroline, we'll get supper all set. Mrs. Taylor's staying on awhile longer too. She'll be in to look after you."

Pa leaned over and kissed his small baby boy on the head. Laura watched him and felt something strong and heartbreaking inside her. She did not know what it was, except that seeing someone with so much love was enough to nearly make her cry. And she was much too big a girl to cry.

With Mrs. Taylor looking after Ma, and Pa tending to the animals in the barn, Laura and Mary and Carrie set about fixing everybody a big dinner. Mary gathered potatoes from the crib in the cellar and peeled and cooked and mashed them up with fresh butter. Laura fried thick slices of salt pork brought from the barrel in the lean-to. They boiled cabbage and onions and set out a bowl of homemade plum preserves. Then they sliced up the thick brown bread Ma had baked on Saturday. The older girls let Carrie help grind the coffee beans in the mill, so Pa could have a good hot cup of coffee to warm his insides when he came back from the barn. And they let Carrie remove the red-checked tablecloth and lay out the tin dishes

and cups and the utensils. Carrie got everything just right.

"Good girl, Carrie," said Mary approvingly.
Mary was already filling in for Ma.

It was a happy supper. Ma couldn't come to
the table, but Pa took a plate of food in to her
and to Mrs. Taylor. Then he joined his girls at
the table. He said the blessing, and when he
blessed everyone at the table, he remembered
especially Ma and their baby boy:

"Thank you, Father, for the pure bundle of
heaven which you have so lovingly sent us.
Bless and keep him and his mother. Bless
them all their days long."

"*Amen,*" said Laura.

"*Amen,*" said Mary.

"*Amen,*" said Carrie.

Then everyone happily ate.

BACK TO THE FARM

W hen spring came, Pa said it was time for the family to move back to Plum Creek, even though some snow still covered the prairie and the streams were shiny with ice. Pa was anxious to get settled on the claim and to start planting. He still did not know for sure whether the grasshoppers would be back, but he was full of hope for a good crop.

Two years earlier a great plague of grasshoppers had descended on the prairie, eating every growing thing as far as the eye could see: every blade of grass, every small flower, every leaf of every tree, every stalk of wheat and ear of corn. Everything. The big bluestem grasses, thick and tall over all the plains, disappeared. The purple prairie clover the cows loved disappeared. All the sunflowers and coneflowers and wild geraniums and violets were gone in a day.

There were so many grasshoppers that when they lit upon trees, the limbs broke under their weight. They ate through the blankets farmers threw over their vegetable patches. They ate window curtains and hoe handles, so hungry and determined were they. The grasshoppers even stopped the great trains of the Union Pacific railroad, for so many of the insects were crushed on the rails that the grease of them set the locomotives' wheels spinning and the trains could not move.

It was a terrible time, but Laura's family had gotten through it. And when the eggs the grasshoppers had laid hatched the following year, Laura and her family had gotten through that, too. Life was hard because the crops were gone and Pa had to go work in the harvesting fields three hundred miles away so their family might have money and food to live on.

Still, the family had found its courage and hope and had endured it all, even as they watched wagon after wagon go back east, some carrying a simple sign on the side that said "Grasshopper." Pa just couldn't give up like that. He couldn't backtrail with everybody else. Not yet. Not until he had nothing at all and no other way to feed his family could Pa give up his land and his prairie to go back east, where there were too many people and too much noise, and where a man just couldn't breathe.

Laura was glad. Laura was like Pa. She never wanted to go back east to all the old towns and old lands. She wanted the new, clean west. She wanted the empty rolling fields of wild grass and the skies full of thousands of birds and the millions of stars shining down every night. Laura was ready to stick it out with Pa, whatever it took.

So in the spring the Ingallses moved out of the rented house in Walnut Grove. They drove their wagon, with their horses Sam and David and their cows Spot and Moon, back to the wonderful house beside Plum Creek, where Pa hoped to grow them some wheat.

Baby Freddie was four months old now, and his three sisters took turns tending him. Sometimes it was hard to take turns, for they all loved him so.

"May I hold Freddie as far as Nelson's?" Mary asked Ma as the girls climbed into the back of the wagon.

"Oh, can't I hold him please this time?" asked Carrie.

Laura wanted to hold Freddie too, but she didn't say anything. She didn't want to make it a squabble.

"Mary asked first," Ma said, "so she may take the baby as far as Nelson's. Then Carrie may hold him as far as the creek. When we cross the water, Laura may hold him until we reach home."

All three girls were happy.

"I will need your help, anyway," said Ma as Laura and her sisters climbed up into the wagon bed. "I have to drive the horses while your pa manages the cows."

Pa had tied the two cows, Spot and Moon, to the rear of the wagon. He stood with a goad in his hand, ready to move them if they got stubborn.

"You take over, flutterbudget," Pa called to Laura, "if Ma doesn't do a good job!"

Laura gave Pa a big smile. Pa knew how much Laura wanted to drive the wagon herself. Laura loved horses.

With Jack trotting underneath as always, and animals in front and in back, the Ingalls wagon pulled away from the little town of Walnut Grove, and headed for farmland two miles north. Though the prairie still lay under an icy, thin layer of snow, already signs of spring were all around. The weedy brown prairie grass was alive with the twitterings of thousands of birds. Some, like the snow buntings that loved to whirl like snowflakes above the fields, had stayed all through the long winter, living on the seeds of the crisp grasses and weeds. Other birds were newly arrived: great flocks of curlews, with their slender curved beaks; sandpipers, with their pretty round heads and long, delicate legs; and those great honkers, the Canada geese, standing hundreds to a field to feed on shattered corn, their graceful black necks and soft brown bodies ready to lift together in an instant with a shock of sound like a great clap of thunder.

Through the snowy open fields, among these busy birds, ran cottontail rabbits, their short brown ears listening for the sound of a redtail hawk overhead. The longer, leaner jackrabbits ran too, their white winter coats turning brown again and their long jackrabbit legs zigzagging through the plains.

Laura loved this world. She loved the tall grasses and the never-ending horizon with not a house or a person in sight. She loved the looming sky, which made everything small and humble. Some pioneers had not known how to live in a world that seemed almost nothing but sky. They felt lost in it.

Not Laura. She felt found.

When the Ingalls wagon finally crossed Plum Creek and made its way up to the wonderful house Pa had built, the whole family breathed a great sigh of relief. Even Jack, still trotting earnestly beneath the wagon, gave a happy bark. This was the nicest house the family had ever lived in, and they had missed it.

"Home!" cried Mary with delight.

"Home," whispered Laura softly to Freddie in her arms. Little Freddie had never seen the wonderful house.

When the family climbed off the wagon and went through the front door with the boughten lock, they saw all their furniture in place, waiting for them. Pa had risen before the sun to bring out the furniture before he brought them.

There was Ma's shiny black cookstove in the kitchen and her rocker alongside. In Ma and Pa's bedroom was their four-poster bed and Freddie's little cradle and even one of Ma's pretty rag rugs on the floor.

"Let's see our room!" Laura said to her sisters, and they all climbed up to the fresh-smelling attic, where their big cozy bed already covered with the straw-tick mattress waited for them.

Laura inhaled deeply.

"This smells like our house," she said with satisfaction.

And by day's end they were all snugly tucked into home. Jack was happy to be on his good horse blanket in the lean-to again.

Spot and Moon were happy to be in the barn, while the horses Sam and David stood at their feed box, munching oats. Freddie's cradle was alongside the warm black stove, and when one of the girls wasn't rocking him, Ma was moving the cradle with her foot while she sewed. Pa, of course, was warming up his fiddle.

"When three little girls are all washed and combed and huddled 'neath their quilts," said Pa, "I'll play us all a nighttime song."

"I'm eleven, Pa," Mary said. "I'm not little anymore."

"Pumpkin pie, you'll always be my little girl," Pa said, his clear blue eyes going crinkly with a smile.

The girls hurriedly washed and dressed for bed. They all wanted to hear Pa's fiddle. Soon they were all three up the ladder, into the chilly attic, and under the great mound of quilts and woolen blankets.

"Shhh," Laura whispered.

Pa's beautiful music began its soft way through the wonderful house. It was an aching, sad sort of music, but happy, too, all at the same time. Laura felt it in her throat. Then Pa began to sing the words:

"Good night to you all, and sweet be thy sleep;
May angels around you their silent watch keep.
Good night, good night, good night, good night."

"Good night, Pa," Laura whispered. And she fell asleep.

RAIN

One of the most wonderful things about the wonderful house was its glass windows. In the sod dugout where Laura's family had first lived on Plum Creek, there had been no glass windows, for there had been no real house. It was just a home scooped from the ground. And before that, in Indian Territory, there wasn't much time to enjoy glass windows, for the family had to pack up and leave that little house. It was sitting on Indian land, and the government had said they must move.

In this wonderful house there were glass windows everywhere: two in the kitchen, two in the big bedroom, and two up in the attic, one on either end. It was out of one of these small windows that Laura first began to watch the cloud grow.

It was about four o'clock on an April afternoon when Laura and Mary were helping Ma clean the house as Carrie kept the baby happy. Mary was downstairs mopping and Laura was upstairs mopping when she felt something different outside. She went to the window to look.

Off to the northwest the sky was turning from a beautiful clear blue to a sullen, ominous black. The blackness was building all along the top of the sky, and closer to the ground a thick dark cloud was moving. As it moved east below the blackness, the cloud grew larger and larger and darker and darker, then—*snap!*—a sudden red streak of lightning fired up its dark face.

All around the house, the prairie land had become eerily calm. Not a bird flew, not a rabbit ran, not a snake slithered. That great dark cloud was bringing a thunderstorm, and all the animals knew it. They had all run home.

"A storm's coming, Ma," Laura called down the ladder.

Ma put down her broom and looked out the kitchen door.

"Goodness," said Ma. "Your pa had better hurry inside. I'll get Jack."

Sam and David were tied up on picket lines outside, and soon Pa had rushed from the field to lead all the animals into the barn.

Pa dashed into the kitchen just as the first hard crack of thunder rattled the pans hanging on the walls.

CrrrrACK!

Laura dropped her mop in the attic and hurried downstairs. Freddie had started crying, Carrie was looking pale, Jack's fur was on end, and outside in the barn one of the cows was bawling.

CrrrACK!

The tin cups shook on their shelf.

"Let's all settle in close to the stove," said Ma, wrapping Freddie close to her and taking

Carrie's hand. "We'll sit out the storm together."

Pa lit the lantern, and they all drew near the warmth of the big range, Carrie on Pa's lap, Ma in the rocker with Freddie, Laura and Mary sharing a bench. Big wet tears rolled down Freddie's quivering face as the sky outside became dark as night and the world let go its spring roar.

Then the mighty rain came, a blinding, heavy sheet of rain so thick that when Laura looked to the window, she could not see through it. The rain washed down so hard, she was afraid it might come through the roof and fill up the wonderful house.

CrrrACK!

"It's a good one!" Pa laughed as he squeezed Carrie closer.

"It's scary," said Mary, pulling her shawl tighter around her shoulders.

"I think it's fun," said Laura. "A little." Now that it began to look as if the house would hold, and Freddie had cried himself into a nice little sleep, Laura had decided to enjoy herself. Laura always loved to be scared, as long as she was safe and Pa was nearby.

For half an hour it rained so hard, Laura's ears nearly hurt from the sound of it. But then the storm began to rumble away to the southeast like a grumpy dog, and a soft, steady splashing of big, slow raindrops stayed behind. Pa got up to look out the door.

"I can hear the creek," he said.

Laura could hear it too. The rain had filled up Plum Creek and set it foaming and roaring. Laura had seen this happen before. The water would be nearly black now and filled with broken tree limbs and sticks and twigs. The banks along the creek would disappear under the water, and the low ground beside the creek would be covered with water as well.

"There won't be anybody crossing that old creek for a while," said Pa. "It's good we have what we need from town."

He turned to Ma.

"What's for supper, Caroline?"

Ma laid soft, sleeping Freddie in his cradle. Carrie gave him a little kiss on the head.

"How does ham and fried potatoes sound?" asked Ma.

"Dee-lightful," said Pa, reaching for his coat on the peg. "I'll go out and make sure the barn's still good and dry. I expect those animals didn't much like all that thunder and roar."

"May I come too, Pa?" Laura asked. She couldn't wait to get out into the wet, bubbling world.

Pa looked at Ma.

"All right, Laura," Ma said. "Mary can help me get supper started. But don't forget, you must finish the mopping as soon as you come back inside."

"Yes, Ma," said Laura, grabbing her coat and a shawl for her head.

"Come on, half-pint," said Pa, pulling open the back door. "Let's see what the storm blew in."

Laura followed Pa outside, and right away she stepped into a big wet puddle. Then she stepped into another, then another, and another. The whole wide world was one wet puddle.

"We might have to row to the barn, half-pint!" said Pa.

Laura laughed. The rain washed across her nose and her cheeks and dripped off the end of her chin. She tasted it with her tongue, and it was clean and sweet.

"Look, Laura, over there!" Pa pointed a

finger to the east, and up in the sky, crossing over the endless, lovely prairie, was Noah's rainbow.

"Pot o' gold out there somewhere," said Pa.

"Really, Pa?" asked Laura.

"Honest truth," answered Pa. "But only elves can find it. That's what they say, anyhow."

"I guess we could sure use a pot of gold, right, Pa?" asked Laura. She knew how hard the grasshoppers had hit.

"Now, flutterbudget," said Pa, putting an arm around her in the rain, "what could a pot of gold possibly bring you that you haven't already got?"

Laura stood next to Pa and looked all around her. She looked at their wonderful house full of real glass windows. She looked at the door leading into it and, beyond that, in her mind, she looked at Ma smiling back at her, and Mary and Carrie and little Freddie all well and happy and safe. She looked down at poor soggy Jack beside her feet and at Pa's old boots, worn from so much work and so many miles to make a good home for his family.

Laura looked at the new barn Pa had built,

warm with the smell of hay and oats and strong, fine animals. She looked through the raindrops at the farmland and fields opening all around, promising wheat and corn and potatoes and good-rooted turnips. And on beyond these were the slender little leaves on the willows beginning to bud and the soft green shoots of the yellow star grass and the blue violets and the friendly white daisies set to bloom.

Laura thought about it all, there in the steady spring rain. Then she looked at Pa.

"You're right, Pa," Laura said with a smile. "I can't think of anything I haven't already got."

Pa hugged her shoulders, and she followed him to the barn.

TERRIBLE SICK

The rain did not stop.
All that evening it rained, and the next day it rained even harder. Mary and Laura and Carrie stayed home from school and watched the rain through the windows. When the wind blew strong, the rain fell nearly sideways from the sky, and as it pinged against the glass, Laura's eyes blinked. It seemed the water would come straight into her face.

The next day it rained even more. Pa went to check the creek and reported a "nasty flood going on"; and he cautioned the girls again about the dangers of the roaring water. Laura knew that danger well. She had already once been nearly swept down the creek, when she was seven years old and foolish. Now she knew better.

Things turned much worse the following day. For as the rain continued, Ma took terribly ill. When Laura woke, she didn't hear Ma down in the kitchen, she didn't smell coffee brewing nor mush frying, she didn't hear Pa coming in from the barn. What Laura heard was Pa's worried voice drifting up from the bedroom downstairs.

"There now, Caroline. There. It's all right now, Caroline. Here, take some tea now."

"Mary, something's wrong," Laura whispered. She and Mary jumped from bed in the dark as Carrie sat straight up, listening.

"Pa!" Mary called down the ladder. "Pa, what is it?"

Pa came to the bottom of the ladder and shushed her.

"Your ma's taken sick, girls," he said. "Get

dressed now. You've got chores."

Laura and Mary and Carrie quickly pulled on their petticoats and dresses and hurried down to Ma's bedroom.

Pa was sitting on a chair at the bedside. Ma was lying in bed, her face to the wall, moaning softly.

"Ma!" cried Carrie. "Ma!" Tears filled her frightened brown eyes.

"Mary, bring me another pan of hot water," said Pa. "Ma's got an awful pain in her side, and she needs these hot cloths. Carrie, you be a big girl and tend to the baby. Laura, you need to see to the animals. Go on, now."

Ma moaned again. She did not turn her head to smile at the girls. She seemed not even to know they were there.

Looking at her, none of the girls moved.

"Hurry!" said Pa.

"Yes, Pa!" they all answered with a jump.

It was a bad morning. Ma seemed to be getting worse, and Pa's face grew more pale and strained. Ma had an awful fever, so Pa put cold cloths on her head while he put hot ones on her side.

The girls were all quiet and tense as they

took care of the chores and little Freddie. Pa hadn't wanted breakfast, or even coffee, so they just nibbled at some bread and lard. The girls weren't hungry either. When work was done, Mary tried to sew and Carrie tried to cut out paper dolls and Laura tried to read. But what they all really were doing was listening to Ma and Pa's every sound.

Suddenly Pa called loudly.

"Laura!"

Laura sprang from her chair and went in to Pa.

"Laura," he said, not looking at her but leaning over Ma, "run to Nelson's quick. Tell Mr. Nelson Ma needs a doctor. Hurry, now!"

Laura gazed at Pa for a moment as she realized what he was telling her to do. Then she said, "Yes, Pa," and she put on her wraps and shoes and ran out of the house.

Outside, the rain was still pouring, and from the yard the dark roar of the raging creek could be heard. Mr. Nelson's house was on the other side of that creek.

Laura ran quickly down the knoll and across the field. The pounding, tumbling creek was so loud, she didn't even hear Jack coming along behind her. Even when he gave two short barks, he sounded very far away.

Laura looked down and saw him. "Hurry, Jack!" she said. They ran together toward the footbridge that crossed to Mr. Nelson's farm. The lowland was so wet, the water covered the tops of Laura's shoes.

When she reached the footbridge, Laura looked out across the black, roiling water. Thick logs were angrily bumping through it, rising and falling with the creek's strong pull. And the water was so high, the footbridge itself was disappearing. Only a small piece of the bridge was visible, far out in the middle of the creek.

"Stay here, Jack!" Laura said. "Stay!"

Jack paced back and forth, whining, the hair on his brindled neck standing straight and stiff.

Laura carefully placed one foot, then the other, in the cold water, feeling for the boards of the bridge. The water already pulled hard at her legs, and she had taken only two steps. Her heart was pounding as the creek rushed around her. But she had to get across! Pa had sent her!

Laura took two more small steps. Then two more. The water was deep now, nearly to her knees, and the feeling of the boards beneath her feet was slipping away. She took two more steps.

"*Laura!*" a voice shouted sharply.

Laura looked up. As she did, she nearly slid away into the flood. She desperately twirled her arms to keep from falling.

"*Laura!*" The voice belonged to Mr. Nelson. He was standing on the bank on the other side of the creek, waving his arms at her.

"*No, Laura, no!*" he called. "*You'll drown! Go back! Go back!*"

Laura brought herself steady. Then with all her strength she shouted, "Ma needs a doctor!"

Mr. Nelson vigorously nodded his head. He pointed in the direction of Walnut Grove. He had understood her.

"All right!" he shouted. "All right! Now go back! Go back!"

Just as Mr. Nelson said this, two large logs came tumbling down the creek and, with a deafening crash, collided in the water in front of him.

"Go home!" he called.

Laura edged carefully backward to the creek bank. When she was out of the water, she grabbed onto Jack's strong neck and caught her shaky breath. Then she hurried back to Ma.

After Laura stepped inside the house and out of her wet coat and shoes and stockings, she walked softly into Ma's bedroom. Pa was still sponging Ma's feverish head. He did not look up when Laura entered.

"Mr. Nelson's going for the doctor, Pa," Laura whispered.

Ma's face was turned toward Pa now, and her eyes looked up at Laura's face, but Ma didn't seem to know her.

"That's good, Laura. That's good," said Pa, continuing to sponge Ma's head.

Suddenly Pa stopped. Holding the cloth in midair, he looked up at Laura.

"The creek," he whispered. His face went white.

"It's all right, Pa," said Laura, and she told him what had happened. She did not tell him how scared she'd been.

Pa put a hand across his eyes and slowly

shook his head. Then he stood up and hugged Laura tight to him.

"I can hear that creek now," Pa said to her. "If I had remembered, I never would have sent you.

"You're a good girl, Laura," Pa said gently.

Laura took a deep, quivering breath. She hoped that doctor would hurry.

THE GOOD DOCTOR

I t was a long wait. Mr. Nelson first had to
ride his horse to the telegraph office in
Walnut Grove. Then he had to send a
message to the town of Redwood Falls, forty
miles away. Then, once the doctor there heard
about Ma, he had to wait for the next train to
Walnut Grove. When he got off the train, Mr.
Nelson had to meet him and drive him out
to the Ingallses' farm. Mr. Nelson also had

to get that doctor across the creek.

But finally, finally, after a long day of Ma's suffering and Freddie's crying and Laura and Mary and Carrie working hard to take care of the cooking, the washing, the trips to the barn, and all the heavyhearted worry they carried inside them . . . finally, late in the evening, the doctor walked through the door. Mr. Nelson was with him, his pant legs soaked and a lantern in his hand. Both he and the doctor were dripping wet.

Pa shook Mr. Nelson's hand, then the doctor's, while the girls stood back shyly.

"You're a good man, Nelson," said Pa.

"Well, I had to rig up a raft to get us across that creek," said Mr. Nelson, "but by golly, we made it."

Pa smiled. He looked very tired.

"Dr. Goodwin," he said, "thank you for coming. My wife has taken terrible sick."

The doctor stood in his wet clothes, holding his wet bag, and he said, "Don't worry, Mr. Ingalls. Let us take a look at her."

Laura gazed at the doctor with gratitude. He had said, *Don't worry, Mr. Ingalls.* That must mean the doctor would make Ma well.

Laura grabbed Carrie's small hand and gave it a squeeze.

Mr. Nelson went back out into the night, though Pa had urged him to stay. Pa told Laura and Mary to fix the doctor a plate of food while he was examining Ma.

"Yes, Pa," they said, and went quickly to work as the doctor disappeared into the bedroom behind Pa. The door closed behind them.

The girls were quiet as they fixed the doctor's supper. It had been such a strange, long day, and now the night felt even stranger. Little Freddie was finally sleeping in his cradle, giving Carrie a rest, too. She had played with him all day. But it was long past her bedtime, and her eyes were tired around the corners and her small mouth had begun to droop.

"Carrie, go on to bed now," said Mary as she sliced up onions and potatoes. "The doctor's going to look after Ma."

Stirring some beans on the stove, Laura looked over at Carrie and saw her heavy eyes and drooping mouth, and Laura smiled and nodded to her.

"Go on, Carrie," said Laura. "Ma's going to be fine."

Carrie was too tired to argue with her big sisters, though she hardly ever argued anyway. She washed and combed and climbed the ladder to bed. Before she went up to the attic, though, she stood in front of Ma's door.

"Night, Ma," Carrie whispered.

Half an hour later, warm food was on the table and Dr. Goodwin and Pa were stepping from the bedroom.

The doctor lifted his nose into the air and breathed deeply.

"My, that food smells good," he said with a big smile. "It is late, and I am hungry."

Sitting down to the table with Pa, Dr. Goodwin rolled back his white cuffs, and he ate and ate and ate. Laura was surprised by how much the doctor ate. He must have seen the surprise on her face.

"I have been living either in a buggy or on a train these past four weeks," he told them. "There's a lot of sickness this spring, and some days I never even take off my shoes. I believe my little girl is going to forget who I am."

Laura had not really thought about doctors

having little girls and taking care of them the way Pa took care of her. She thought about the doctor's little girl watching out the window for him.

"She won't forget you," said Laura. "She will think of you all the days long."

Everyone looked at Laura, and she blushed a little. Laura was usually shy with strangers. But tonight she was weary and the doctor was kind and she could not be so careful in the things she said.

When the men finished eating, Laura and Mary cleared the table and began the washing up.

"When you're all done, girls, you go on up to bed," said Pa. "Dr. Goodwin will stay the night, and one of us will watch Ma while the other sleeps on the floor. She will be well looked after."

Laura and Mary nodded. They knew Ma was in good hands.

Upstairs in bed, her head on her feather pillow and her eyes looking up toward the rafters and on, in her mind, to the white shining stars in the sky, Laura said a silent prayer for her ma.

WORK AND WORRY

The next morning Ma was still very ill. And Dr. Goodwin had other patients he must get to, so he could not stay longer. After breakfast Pa put on his coat to take the doctor across the creek to Nelson's. Mr. Nelson would take the doctor back to the train.

As Pa spoke quietly with the doctor about how to care for Ma and how often to give the powders the doctor had mixed together, Laura carefully peeped into Ma's bedroom.

Ma was sleeping. Laura could see her face, and it looked yellow, yellow as a daisy's heart. Laura was frightened. She went back to Pa.

"Pa?" she whispered to him as the doctor pulled on his coat. "Pa, why is Ma yellow?"

Pa patted the top of her head.

"Her liver is the trouble, Laura. A sick liver makes a person yellow."

Mary and Carrie, wiping the breakfast dishes in the kitchen, stopped and listened, wide-eyed.

Dr. Goodwin put on his hat and smiled at the girls.

"I will be back in two days to look after your ma again," he said. "The best you can do for her is give her rest. Can you do that?"

The girls all nodded.

"Yes, sir," said Mary.

"I'll be right back," said Pa, opening the door.

When he closed it behind him and the doctor, Laura looked at Mary, and Carrie looked at them both. To Laura the whole house felt empty, though they were all in it, all except Pa, and he would be right back.

Freddie was in his cradle and Ma was in bed, and Laura and her sisters were standing in the kitchen, yet still the house felt abandoned, as if a family had once lived there but they had all moved away, taking everything with them and shutting the door.

It was Monday, wash day.

"We have to do the washing," said Mary. "We'll just hang the clothes to dry in the lean-to if the rain doesn't stop."

Laura nodded. She was actually glad it was wash day. She wanted hard work to do, not the quiet of sewing and mending. It seemed as if the quiet would eat everything up.

The rain had softened some, though the creek still roared. Laura grabbed two buckets and started for the spring to fill them up. It might take a little longer at the spring than at the creek, but it would be safer. Mary added wood to the fire, to set the wash water boiling.

When Pa returned, a pot of white clothes was boiling on the stove, and in another pot the soaped-up, dirtier clothes were soaking. Pa's clothes always needed a long soaking, for they were always muddy. After the soaking

Mary and Laura would carry the clothes into the lean-to and take turns beating them on a bench with a battling stick, to loosen the dirt even more before the clothes were rubbed on a washboard and rinsed.

It was hard, heavy work for two young girls without their ma.

Dr. Goodwin kept his promise, and two days later he was at their door again. Again he stayed the night and left the next morning. He promised to be back in three days.

Ma was very, very thin and still yellow. Everyone was afraid. Pa was grim and silent. The girls were quiet all day long, trying to do the many chores Ma had done, and some of Pa's, too. And Jack stayed faithfully beside Ma's bedroom door day and night.

The rains still came and the creek still roared. The women from church wouldn't come to help the family, Pa said, because they were afraid of the creek. Even Mrs. Nelson was afraid. Only Pa and Mr. Nelson and the doctor were brave enough to cross it for Ma.

And they crossed the creek many times. Dr. Goodwin came to see Ma again and again and again. Finally, after days of living in a house that was so hushed by sickness that Laura wondered if her family would ever remember how to laugh and sing again . . . after so many days and so much worry, Dr. Goodwin finally stood at the door and spoke the words they were all waiting to hear.

"She will live," he said.

Mary and Laura looked at each other, and tears ran from their eyes and splashed down onto their dresses.

It took a few weeks more, but finally Ma was well enough to sit up in her rocker. And she wasn't yellow anymore.

"You don't look so much like my sunflower that bends and nods in the breeze," said Pa, smiling and smoothing Ma's hair.

Carrie sat like a good girl by Ma's side all day. And Jack was so glad whenever Ma sat in her rocker that he jumped happily into the air, then turned around and around and around before he laid his head on her feet.

Ma was always saying, "You are all too good to me!"

But Laura wished to do even more for Ma. She wished she could give Ma everything.

Laura never again wanted to think about Ma being sick and thin and yellow and not knowing who her own little girl was.

Ma was well again. And as Pa always liked to say, "All's well that ends well."

A BLASTED
COUNTRY

It was late May now on the tall-grass
prairie, and a wildflower quilt had been
spread all over the fertile, flat land. The
tall purple heads of four-o'clocks swayed
constantly in the never-ending breeze, and
yellow-orange forget-me-nots bloomed on the
banks of Plum Creek. The small white flowers of wild strawberries were opening, and
every afternoon Laura and her sisters went
walking across the meadows, spreading wide

the grasses and looking between them for sweet, ripe red berries to pop into their mouths. They often took little Freddie along. Laura and Mary took turns carrying him on their hips, and they showed him the world in which he would grow up.

"See, Freddie, these are pussytoes," said Laura one day, pulling up a short, fuzzy white flower. "See the little kitty foot?" She tickled his nose with the soft "paw" of the flower. Freddie laughed and rubbed his face with his tiny hand. Freddie wasn't chubby and round like other babies. He had always been thin, and sometimes he got a fever, which worried Ma and Pa.

But to his sisters he was a beautiful boy, and they had things to show him.

Carrie brought him a handful of yellow flowers.

"Buttercups, Freddie," she said. Carrie loved buttercups. When she was smaller, she tried to eat them because she thought they would taste like butter. But now she knew not to. Now she knew just to look at them.

"Don't eat buttercups, Freddie," she said with a smile.

The prairie was full of snakes, but the girls knew not to try to bring one of those to Freddie. Most snakes were nice. But some were poisonous. The prairie-dog towns were often full of snakes, and the girls never went poking sticks around the mounds of the prairie-dog tunnels.

But there were small gray mice to watch, running through the fields. And voles eating the roots and seeds of thick grasses. And, of course, always the birds—buntings and juncoes and wrens and orioles and grackles and doves—thousands of birds singing thousands of songs in the clear, blue open air.

The girls had a lovely walk this day with the baby. As they were returning home, both Laura and Mary slapped at something on their hands at the same time. Then Carrie slapped at something on her face. Then with a soft flutter of small green wings, something landed on Freddie's foot.

It was a young grasshopper.

"Oh, no," said Laura, flicking it away. The girls hurried back home. They saw Pa out walking in his newly planted hay field. He was walking very slowly, and he stopped now and again to bend over and look at something on the ground.

"Oh, no," said Mary.

That was the beginning of that summer's grasshoppers. They were back. Laura looked at all the bright green and yellow and pink and orange and purple around her. She knew that in a week, all the living plants would be gone.

And they were. That was when Pa finally gave up.

"I'll not stay another day in this blasted country," he said.

Laura knew Pa wanted to stay. And he might have stayed, really, if he knew a way to make it work. But again Pa would have no crops this year. He had a large debt of doctor bills, and even though the doctor had told Pa not to worry, to pay him when he could, Pa didn't like to be beholden to any man. And Pa also owed money to the lumberyard for the sawn wood and the boughten doors and the sweet pine floors and the real glass windows of the wonderful house. He had counted on this year's wheat crop to pay for all that. He had believed that two years of fighting grasshoppers would be as much as any fate might ask of him.

But now Pa had nothing. And he could not leave Ma, with three little girls and a baby, to go off east for many months and work another farmer's fields.

Laura knew that Pa was thinking of the family backtrailing, maybe all the way back east to Wisconsin. And, oh, how Laura hoped they wouldn't. She wouldn't feel free there, she was sure of it.

So when Pa said one evening after supper, "Caroline, I've made some plans," Laura felt the worry tighten up all through her. She waited quietly with her sisters for Pa to speak.

"Mr. Keller in town has agreed to buy the farm," Pa said.

"Oh, Charles," said Ma.

Laura felt the sting of tears in her eyes. But she would not cry. She knew she mustn't. Pa might make her leave the table.

"And I've an offer of a job," continued Pa. "It's the best hope I can see for us all."

Pa then explained that Mr. Steadam, a friend from church, had given up farming and had traded for a hotel in Iowa in a town called Burr Oak. Mr. Steadam had asked Pa to join him in running this hotel, with Ma and Mrs. Steadam taking care of the cooking and cleaning.

Laura could see the worn look on Ma's face. She could not imagine Ma having to do more work than she already managed every day.

But all Ma said was "If you think it's best, Charles, we will go."

Two days later, at sunrise, the family was saying good-bye to the wonderful house. Laura swallowed back her tears as she helped pack the clothes and quilts and dishes into the wagon. Laura could not watch as Pa took down the carved wooden bracket and the beautiful china shepherdess. She turned away as Ma took down the pretty white curtains with calico trim.

Laura had always loved moving on, following the sun setting in the west, leading her farther and farther into an open, unsettled country.

But this time they would be traveling east and south, to Iowa. And they would have no farm of their own to look forward to, no wonderful house, no horizon of orange and pink and blue to gaze at from their own front door after supper.

They would be in someone else's house, in an old town settled a long time ago. A town that didn't need any pioneers.

As Laura helped Pa load the flour and cornmeal and beans and sugar into the wagon, she asked in a small, quiet voice, "Pa, will Jack always stay with us?"

Pa smiled at her.

"Of course, flutterbudget," he said, lifting the flour barrel up and into the wagon bed. "What would this family do without a good watchdog?"

"Even in a hotel?" asked Laura.

"Hotels need watching too," said Pa.

Laura let out a deep breath and felt something let go a little in her chest. With Jack watching, maybe things would be all right.

THE
BEEKEEPER'S
HOUSE

By the time the golden-yellow sun was halfway up the sky, the Ingalls family was traveling out of sight of the wonderful house. Laura and Mary and Carrie sat in the back of the wagon and watched the house shrink smaller and smaller on the horizon. In the barn, which was only a dot now on the seam of earth and sky, they knew Moon was waiting for her new owner, Mr. Keller, to take her down by the creek. Pa said the family could manage only one cow in Iowa, so they kept Spot. Laura wondered if Moon would be watching for Spot all day, not knowing Spot had left behind the barren fields of Plum Creek. Laura already missed Moon.

It was a sunny spring day, and as Sam and David pulled the wagon carefully over the dusty, rutted road—with Spot behind and Jack below—Laura could not help feeling her heart lift in spite of everything. She knew it would be beautiful in Iowa, where there would be healthy green-leaved trees and sweet open flowers and pretty birds in the air. And really all that ever mattered to Laura, anyway, was her family. As long as Ma and Pa and Mary and Carrie and little Freddie were near her and with her, she was home. Even if she had to live in a wagon the rest of her life, Laura would be happy if her family lived there, too.

And there was something good to look forward to, for they were on their way first to Uncle Peter and Aunt Eliza's house in South Troy, Minnesota. Uncle Peter was Pa's brother, and he had written and told Pa to bring the family to his farm for the summer. Pa could work the fields there until it was time to go to Iowa in November. Pa thought this was a fine idea, and so did Ma, for Aunt Eliza was Ma's own sister, and Ma always wanted to see her. Uncle Peter and Aunt Eliza had five children, and they were not only Laura's cousins, they were Laura's *double* cousins, because Pa's brother and Ma's sister had married.

"Do you remember," Laura asked Mary as the wagon moved along, "the Christmas we spent with Uncle Peter and Aunt Eliza and the cousins in Wisconsin?"

Mary smiled and nodded.

"We made snow pictures," she said. "And pancake men for breakfast."

Carrie looked over at them.

"Where was I?" she asked.

Mary touched her finger to the tip of Carrie's nose.

"You were just a baby then," said Mary. "The newest angel. You don't remember Wisconsin."

"Will the cousins mind that I'm big now?" asked Carrie.

"Oh, no," said Mary. "They'll be happy you can play with them. And anyway, there are two new cousins Laura and I haven't even met. In Wisconsin there were only—"

"Alice, Peter, and Ella," finished Laura.

"Don't interrupt, Laura," Mary reminded her. "But now," she continued, "there is also Edith—who is little, like you—and Lansford, who is a baby, like Freddie."

Carrie's face brightened.

"Lansford and Freddie are the newest angels now," she said.

"Yes." Mary smiled.

At midday Pa pulled the wagon beside a grove of bare trees with a fresh stream nearby so the family could eat and the horses could rest and drink. Ma braided the girls' hair before she let them have their hardtack and tea.

"Girls must have their hair combed and braided before dinner," she said.

After a short rest the family climbed back into the wagon and was off again. Pa wanted to travel as far as he could this first day, for the weather was so fine.

But later, as the light of day began to dim and the horizon washed all dark and light pinks against the deep-blue sky, Pa began watching for a good place to camp for the night. Laura could see a small farmhouse off to the south.

"Let's make camp over near that farmer's land, Caroline," said Pa. "We'll stay far enough away not to be intruding while we make use of the water that's bound to be near those trees."

"It looks a fine place to stop, Charles," said Ma. "And we are all ready to stand on our legs awhile."

Pa drove the wagon to a nice flat patch of earth near the farmer's trees. There was no green grass nor flowers anywhere. Laura and her sisters jumped from the wagon. The air was so cool and fresh, Laura couldn't wait to go playing in the stream.

"No playing in the stream, girls," Ma said, handing Freddie to Pa before she stepped down from the wagon seat. "It is too late, and we must get supper."

Laura gave a deep sigh. *Oh, well,* she thought, *at least we're out of the wagon.*

While Pa tended the horses, Laura and Mary lifted the box of dishes and the skillet and teakettle and coffee pot. Ma took Carrie and Freddie for a little walk, and Jack trotted along with them. Carrie held tight to Ma's hand and skipped along beside her. Laura watched her little sister.

"It's not so long ago Carrie was the baby of the family," Laura said to Mary.

Mary smiled.

"There are always new babies," she said.

Laura looked at Carrie and was glad Carrie got to hold Ma's hand. Carrie still needed to be the baby sometimes.

The sun had gone down when the family finally sat to eat their supper, and the air was softly gray. Ma passed out plates of fried mush and boiled turnips and round white pieces of hardtack. They were all eating and watching the fireflies light up the farmer's fields when out of the dusky light stepped two little girls. They had a pan of something in their hands. Jack gave a short, sharp bark, but his fur didn't stand up. Jack knew they were children.

"Well, welcome!" called Pa. "Come join us!"

The little girls walked shyly over to the campfire.

"Our ma thought you might like a pan of

gingerbread," said the older girl.

"My goodness," said Ma, taking the pan as Jack stood between them, sniffing it. "How very kind of her!"

"Smells delicious," said Pa.

The little girls smiled happily.

Pa introduced the family, and the girls said their names were Elizabeth and Annabelle. Laura thought that Annabelle was a lovely name.

"Our ma and pa asked if you'd like to come visit," said Elizabeth.

"We wouldn't want to be any trouble," said Ma.

"It's no trouble," said Elizabeth. "Ma likes company."

So Pa tied Jack to the wagon to watch it, and the Ingalls family followed the little girls across the farmer's pasture to visit. The man and his wife were waiting on the porch to greet them.

"Welcome, travelers!" said the farmer, shaking Pa's hand and introducing his wife to Ma. They were the Wilsons. And soon, sitting on the front porch and listening to the grown-ups talk awhile, Laura found out that

Mr. Wilson was a beekeeper.

"They are charming little creatures, those bees," said Mr. Wilson. "Working with them does a man good. They need nothing more than a field of flowers and well-kept hives and they are happy. They're good little workers, too. In the hot summers, I have even seen them take turns lining up and fanning their wings to cool the hives."

Mr. Wilson smiled at Laura and her sisters.

"Flowers and bees cannot exist one without the other," he said.

Laura had never thought of this as every summer she had gazed at the vast flower fields alive with the hummings of thousand of bees. But what of this summer? And the one before?

"There aren't any flowers now, Mr. Wilson," said Laura. "What will the bees do?"

The smile left Mr. Wilson's face, and he shook his head sadly.

"When the hoppers ate away all the flowers," he said, "the bees could make no honey to feed their young."

He sighed.

"So they stung their babies to death and

carried them all out of the hives."

Laura and Mary both gave a little gasp.

Mr. Wilson shook his head again and looked over at Pa.

"We're packing up, too, Mr. Ingalls," he said. "Heading back to Kentucky. I just don't want to live another day in a country where not even a bee can make a living."

Laura watched as Pa nodded his head in sympathy. Pa knew plenty about not being able to make a living.

Later, washed and combed and tucked into the wagon bed beside her sisters, Laura heard Pa take out his fiddle for one round of song before sleep. The moon hung high in the sky, and with the wagon flaps open, Laura could see its white light resting on the bare branches of the trees, as if to comfort and cover them. She could not help thinking about those baby bees.

Pa must have been thinking about them too, for the sound of his bow on the fiddle strings was plaintive and questioning. Pa played this questioning music awhile, letting its voice rise up to the stars. Then his tune changed over to a lullaby. And he sang:

"Sleep, my child, and peace attend thee
All through the night.
Guardian angels God will send thee
All through the night.
Soft the drowsy hours are creeping,
Hill and vale in slumber sleeping,
I my loving vigil keeping
All through the night."

Laura felt a small tear in the corner of her eye. She wasn't sure why it was there.

But she knew she had needed that lullaby.

"Night, Pa," she said.

"Night, little half-pint," Pa answered softly.

A REUNION

When Laura and her family finally saw in the distance the farm belonging to *another* Ingalls family, they were all feeling much better. The world was green and alive again, for grasshoppers had not been in this part of Minnesota. And the excitement of seeing their relatives had helped everyone along. Already Ma was talking about picking some pears with Aunt Eliza to make preserves, and Pa was talking about helping

Uncle Peter build that henhouse he'd been thinking about. The girls just wanted to play with their cousins.

When Pa stopped the horses, the door of the farmhouse flew open.

"Uncle Charles! Aunt Caroline!" called Alice, the first cousin through the door.

"Laura, Mary!" called Peter, the second.

"Carrie!" called Edith, the third. Edith had not met Carrie or Laura or Mary before. But it was easy to tell which girl in the wagon was Carrie, for Carrie was the littlest.

Out from the barn came Uncle Peter, and out from the kitchen came Aunt Eliza and the baby, and running from the garden came Ella, the last cousin.

So much family! There were so many Ingallses hugging each other in Uncle Peter's yard that Laura could hardly believe it. They all laughed and talked and passed the babies from arm to arm, and Carrie said, "It feels like Christmas."

Pa patted the top of her bonnet. "And we just got ourselves *seven* special presents!"

Carrie quickly counted the members of Uncle Peter's family. Then she smiled.

It did not take many days for the two families to settle themselves into a shared house. Uncle Peter and Aunt Eliza had a fine family home. They had been living there for enough years to make the place seem old and beloved. Gooseberry bushes had been gathered from the woods and planted in neat rows along the sides of the wooden farmhouse, and a small grove of wild plums had been transplanted in the back. Aunt Eliza and the children had made a small garden near the kitchen door, and this was planted with yellow squash, cabbages, corn, melons, tomatoes, and shiny green beans.

The house also had its own cellar dug just outside the pantry door. Steps cut into the dirt walls led down into it, and here Laura and her sisters were amazed by the bounty of food. Forty bushels of potatoes and dozens of bushels of apples, onions, cabbages, carrots, and beets filled many deep bins. On shelves against the wall stood rows and rows of canned fruits— cherries, gooseberries, plums, and pears, all put up in tin cans and sealed with wax. There were rows of pickles: cucumber pickles and tomato pickles, pickled apples and pickled pigs' feet.

And on the floor stood heavy stone jars filled with lard and covered with cloths.

Supper was a large affair, with nine children now to feed, and the families took turns at the table, spooning onto their plates fried cakes and stewed chicken, sausage and mashed potatoes, roast spare ribs. For dessert there were cherry and gooseberry pies or Aunt Eliza's famous pound cake.

Once supper was over, everyone wandered outside to watch the sun set and the flashing fireflies come out. The earthy smell of plowed fields was all around them, and the cousins lay on the grass and watched the stars come out in the fading blue sky while Pa played his tunes on the fiddle.

Everyone shared in the chores as well. The older girls, Mary and Alice, preferred helping Ma and Aunt Eliza with the cooking and cleaning and caring for the two little babies. Uncle Peter and Pa went off to work the crops every morning at dawn. Carrie and Edith played close to home. And Laura and Ella and Peter were left with the chore of watching Uncle Peter's cows all day.

But to Laura this was no chore at all. Every

morning she helped Ella and Peter turn the cows out of the barn and drive them to their pasture along the beautiful Zumbro River. Day was dawning, and as she walked across the dewy green grass in her bare feet, Laura watched the soft gray horizon turn purple, then pink, then orange, and soon up came the trembling golden sun, setting every blade of grass shimmering. The cows wandered happily ahead, their bells lightly ringing; the birds sang clearly and with joy; and all through the morning air drifted the aroma of honeysuckle and cherries and sweet wild plums.

Late in the day the three cousins went back to get the cows. They listened for the *tinkle-tinkle-tinkle* of the bells, which would tell where to find them. The plum thickets along the river were heavy now with big, juicy plums. Laura and Ella and Peter loved to stop to eat up as many as they could, and sometimes they became so involved in their eating, they forgot all about the cows!

Tinkle-tinkle-tinkle-tinkle.

"Oh no!" Peter would cry. "The cows are going home without us!"

And the children would drop the soft,

dripping plums from their hands and run to *follow* the cows home instead of *leading* them.

"You are bringing those cows home much too late," Pa would scold.

"Yes, Pa," Laura would answer, never revealing that the cows really had brought her home.

Things seemed almost perfect at Uncle Peter's farm, with nice cousins to play with, wonderful fresh fruits and garden vegetables to eat every day, the gentle laughter of Ma and Aunt Eliza in the kitchen, and the affectionate brotherly joking between Pa and Uncle Peter arriving from the fields.

But things were not completely perfect. Because little Freddie would not stay well.

For most of the spring and summer the baby had had bouts of sickness. He often wouldn't eat, and sometimes he was feverish and soiled diaper after diaper. Ma would give him dandelion tea and Bower's Infant Cordial from her medicine box. He would begin to be well, and everyone would stop worrying. Then he would grow sick again. He stayed thin and restless and pale, and Ma didn't like to let him out of her sight. She rarely let the girls carry him far.

Finally Freddie worried them so that Pa called for a doctor. He came from another town, just as Dr. Goodwin had come to see Ma at Plum Creek. The doctor examined Freddie inside the house while the children all stayed outside. And when he left, the doctor did not look at them. Not at Laura or Mary or Carrie or any of the cousins. He just stepped into his buggy and drove away.

Laura watched the buggy rolling down the road, and a cold, hard hurt filled her chest. The doctor had not looked at them. He had not said their baby would be better.

LITTLE FREDDIE

F reddie died at the end of August. Pa made a casket for him, and they buried him on Uncle Peter's farm. Uncle Peter bought a small white tombstone, and on it he wrote:

CHARLES FREDERICK INGALLS
1875–1876
Too sweet a bud to bloom on earth

For the rest of the summer the family took turns visiting Freddie. Ma was out with him the most. Every afternoon she put on a clean apron and a bonnet and she walked out the door and across the field, gathering flowers along the way. She liked to go alone, but sometimes she allowed one of the girls to go with her.

This day it was Laura's turn. She washed and combed and tied on her bonnet. Then she went with Ma.

They did not say anything as they walked through the grasses under the hot September sun. There were no words for the sadness they felt.

When they reached Freddie's little grave, they each bent down and laid their bouquets of wildflowers for him. Ma bowed her head and closed her eyes. Laura watched as a flock of great blue herons crossed the sky.

"He was an angel, Ma," Laura said softly.

"Yes, he was," answered Ma.

And, holding hands, they turned and walked home.

BURR OAK, IOWA

In early November, in a cold, constant rain, it was time for Laura and her family to leave their good relatives and drive south into Iowa. The fields had been harvested, the gardens emptied. Pa had built a henhouse. Ma had canned some pears. And together they had buried their boy. It was time to go.

Uncle Peter and Aunt Eliza and all the cousins stood on the porch, saying their farewells to Laura's family and giving them small

things for their trip. Aunt Eliza had made a
fresh pan of corn bread for them. The cousins
had put together a reticule each for Mary and
Laura, with new blocks of nine-patch inside to
sew. For Carrie they had made a sock doll.

"We will miss you," said Uncle Peter, shaking Pa's hand.

"Come back and see us very soon," said
Aunt Eliza, giving Ma a good, long hug.

Pa and Ma climbed up on the wagon seat,
and Laura and her sisters climbed into the
wagon bed. Spot was tied behind. Sam and
David stood brushed and ready to go. And

Jack listened underneath, waiting for Pa to flick the reins.

"Good-bye!"

"Good-bye!"

Uncle Peter and his family waved a long, long time as the Ingalls wagon slowly rolled away. Laura knew, looking out of the back of the wagon, what everyone was thinking. She knew who was being left behind. But she tried not to let her mind dwell on it. She didn't search the fields to the east for the small white tombstone. She couldn't.

As the family rolled farther south, the weather grew worse. "Blasted rain," said Pa. Everyone felt unhappy.

Then, late in the day, in an especially heavy downpour, the way became so thick with mud that Sam and David stopped pulling the wagon and refused to go another step.

"Come on, boys! Come on!" Pa yelled from the wagon seat. He snapped the whip a few times, but the horses wouldn't move.

"Hold the reins, Caroline," said Pa. Laura and her sisters watched as he stepped out into the rain over the dashboard and along the shaft to take hold of the horses' heads.

"I'll pull, Caroline!" Pa called, water dripping off his wet beard. "You urge them on!"

Ma called out to the horses while Pa pulled.

"Giddap!" called Ma, flicking the reins. "Giddap!"

Sam and David were good horses. They couldn't ignore Pa while he was standing right before their faces.

They gave a hard pull. But the wagon was so deep inside a mud hole, it rolled back.

The horses pulled again.

"Good boys!" called Pa. "Good!"

But the wagon rolled back.

The horses pulled a third time.

"There you go!" shouted Pa. "Good boys!"
Finally the wagon was out of the hole.

And it was like that all the way to Burr
Oak. Mud holes, a cold, pouring rain, and
independent-minded horses. Poor Jack was
so muddy, Laura could barely see the brindle
on him. Only Spot seemed unconcerned and
chewed her hay calmly as the water fell off
her back.

Each night when the family camped, the
ground was too wet to build a fire, so Ma
sliced some cold boiled potatoes and turnips
and thick pieces of bread with preserves to
eat. Everyone squeezed together in the back
of the wagon and had supper. Ma had taken to
reading aloud from the Bible every night, and
she began one of the Psalms as the rain fell all
around them:

"God be merciful unto us, and bless us; and
cause his face to shine upon us; that thy way
may be known upon earth. . . ."

Ma read softly for a while, and when she

was finished, Carrie asked, "Will you play your fiddle, Pa?"

"When we're out underneath the sky again," Pa said. "I need a little elbow room to make music."

So the family settled down to sleep to the tune of a lonely wolf, not a fiddle, as Jack bristled under the wagon boards and growled into the night.

Finally, after a cold, wet journey of many days—many more than Pa had anticipated— they reached the town of Burr Oak. It was nearly evening.

Burr Oak, Iowa, sat on a softly rolling plain, and all around it Laura could see the many scattered groves of tall trees. The town itself, she could tell, was nothing like Walnut Grove. Walnut Grove had been a new town, with only two small stores, a blacksmith's, and a schoolhouse. Burr Oak had many more buildings, and most of them were made of old, weathered brick, not new-sawn wood. Laura saw a livery, a harness shop, a creamery, a blacksmith's, a doctor's office, two general stores, a tin shop, and two hotels just on the main street alone. There were other streets leading to other buildings, too.

Mary pointed to a tall white building where several wagons, including a stagecoach, sat out front.

"Is that our hotel, Pa?" she asked.

"No," said Pa. "That's the American House hotel. Ours is that smaller one up ahead. The Burr Oak House."

Mary and Laura and Carrie all squeezed together behind Ma and Pa to look. Ahead they saw a white wooden building sitting on a sloping hill. It had a low-slung roof over a wide front porch and a split-rail fence running along beside and behind it. There were big glass windows of six-over-six upstairs and down.

Pa brought the wagon to a stop in front of it.

"Caroline," he said, looking over at Ma, "I believe this is our new home."

Ma smiled bravely at Pa.

"It will be fine," she said.

Laura and Mary exchanged glances. They hoped so.

THE STEADAM BOYS

The Burr Oak House was a pretty place. By the end of her first week there, Laura still wasn't sure she was ever going to like living in it. But the hotel did have a comfort and charm.

There were two doors on the big front porch, one leading into the hotel parlor, the other leading into the hotel saloon. Ma said the girls must never walk into the saloon. Laura could hear the men's cursing, loud voices, and card playing, and she didn't want to go in there anyway.

But she liked the hotel parlor. It was so homelike. It had a pretty round rug on the floor, decorated with leaves and berries, and pretty flowered paper on its walls. A lace-covered table with claw-and-ball legs sat in one corner, and beside it were two small chairs with red velvet seats. Laura loved to touch that velvet.

Taking up most of the other side of the room was a magnificent Bent parlor organ. It was made of dark polished mahogany, and its tall ornate mantel reached nearly to the ceiling. Clean white keys glistened above a filigreed panel bearing a carved heart in the center, and next to the organ was an oak secretary holding stacks and stacks of sheet music ready to be played.

When Mary first saw this organ, she cried, "Oh, what a beautiful organ!" Laura knew how much Mary wished for music lessons. They all knew it. But Pa could not afford lessons. Pa did the best he could.

Off to the side of the parlor was the small hotel office where Pa and Mr. Steadam handled the business. Pa kept his fiddle in this room, and he picked it up and played it when he could, filling the whole place with gladness.

Behind the parlor was a big bedroom that was always rented by a wealthy man named Mr. Bisbee. Mr. Bisbee owned a lot of property in town, but he preferred living in a hotel.

Upstairs were four small sleeping rooms. One of these belonged to the Steadams, and the other three were reserved for travelers.

Downstairs was the big kitchen and the dining room. The kitchen had both a large black range and a fireplace with a crane at one end for hanging cooking pots. Floor-to-ceiling cabinets were filled with all manner of bowls and pots and cups and dishes and utensils. There were five big barrels of flour and wide chests filled with coffee and sugar and baking powder and salt.

The dining room had a very long wooden table with long benches pulled up to it, and it could seat about twenty people. A pine sideboard for holding extra bowls of food and water pitchers stood against the wall, under the window. The hotel's guests and anyone else who paid a quarter would be served breakfast, dinner, or supper here, cooked up by Ma and Mrs. Steadam.

Also downstairs, just off the dining room, was the bedroom where Laura and her family slept. It was not a very big room, and it had just enough space for a four-poster with curtains around it for Ma and Pa, and a smaller trundle for the three girls. Ma had laid their own quilts and pillows on their beds, but everything else that made a place theirs—the little china shepherdess, Laura's teacup jewel box, Carrie's brown-and-white china dog—these things Ma had left packed away. She had said there just wasn't room enough for them. But without them Laura felt as unrooted as all the travelers passing through.

Jack and Spot and Sam and David were all living in the hotel barn. Jack was at first not too happy about it, but Pa had a long talk with him and Jack stopped whining. Laura made a nice bed for Jack in the old organ crate, and she and the girls went out and played with him often. Jack knew never to stray, so Pa didn't have to tie him, as long as he was good.

The only people at the hotel Jack didn't much like were the Steadam boys, Johnny and

Ruben. They made Jack's hair stand up. When Johnny had first met Laura and Mary, he had said to them, "I'm Johnny Steadam and I'm a holy terror." He was pretty much right.

The boys were rowdy and loud, and worse, they liked to tease girls. When Laura walked from the kitchen up to the parlor, Johnny liked to hide behind the door at the top of the stairs and yank her braid as she passed through.

"Ouch!" Laura yelled. Johnny laughed and laughed. Laura wanted so much to pinch him hard, but she knew Ma would never forgive her. One of Johnny's legs was a little shorter than the other, so he had to wear a block of wood under his foot, strapped to that leg. Because of this, Ma had instructed the girls never to be mean to him.

"But he's mean to us, Ma," Laura had said.

"And you are a lady," answered Ma, and that ended the discussion.

Ruben was given to stealing things. When Carrie's sock doll, Bessie, disappeared, Laura was sure Ruben had her somewhere. When she got the chance, Laura sneaked into the Steadams' room to look for her. Laura knew she was being very bad, going into someone else's room. But Carrie was her little sister, and if Laura must protect her, then she must protect Bessie, too.

The room was a mess. It was nothing like Ma's nice, clean home-keeping. Clothes were flung into all the corners, the beds were rumpled, and parts of broken toys were scattered everywhere. Laura had promised herself she would not open any drawers. But she would look around the room for any small sign of Bessie.

And sure enough, just peeking over the top of a boy's dirty boot, she saw Bessie's sewn black eyes. Bessie had been looking for Laura, too.

Laura snatched Bessie, then went to find Carrie. The weather was snowy now, and Carrie, bundled up and with Jack beside her, was outside, watching the snowflakes drop into the little pond behind the hotel. Laura put on her coat and walked down the hill. She smiled as she approached Carrie and put a finger over her lips, which was their signal for secrets. Then she slipped Bessie into Carrie's hands.

Carrie's brown eyes widened and a big, happy smile spread across her face.

"Hide her," whispered Laura. "Ruben stole Bessie, and he'll steal her again."

Carrie's face became serious, and nodding, she tucked Bessie into her pocket.

"Our secret?" whispered Laura.

"Yes," whispered Carrie.

Laura drew a satisfied breath. That was one win over the Steadam boys.

Mr. Reid's Scholars

The Burr Oak schoolhouse was an old stone building standing beneath a large grove of trees on a hillside just east of State Street. It was a short walk from the Burr Oak House, and Ma sent Laura and her sisters there as soon as they had settled into the routine of the hotel and could be spared from some of the work. Laura and Mary still had to serve breakfast to the earliest guests before going on to school. But the girls were used to rising before the sun, and as long as they knew they would soon escape the day's long hours of cooking and cleaning, Laura and Mary were content. It was harder for Laura to wait on tables than for Mary, for Laura so dreaded meeting strangers, and of course the hotel was full of them. But she smiled at all those she met and kept their plates full and their coffee hot, and no one ever guessed how nervous she felt.

But she was not nervous at all in the new school she attended, and this had everything to do with Mr. Reid.

Mr. Reid was a young schoolmaster who had moved from Decorah to Burr Oak to teach for the winter term. Because the big farm boys often came into town in winter for their schooling, after the harvesting was done, many towns wanted men, not women, to teach them. Most of the big boys were actually not boys at all, but grown-ups, and they could be coarse and rough and too much for a young woman to handle. Schoolteaching was not a job many men wanted, for it did not last all year and they could not support a family on a small eight-month salary. But sometimes a very young man could be persuaded to teach just through the winter, until he went on to a more permanent occupation.

When Laura first saw her new teacher standing at the door of the schoolhouse, her mouth flew open in surprise.

"Why, Mr. Reid!" she said.

Mary, beside her, gave her a nudge.

"Laura, your manners," said Mary.

Carrie held Mary's hand and smiled happily up at Mr. Reid.

"You live at our hotel," said Carrie.

Mr. Reid smiled with pleasure.

"Yes, I do," he agreed. "And your name, I believe, is Carrie."

Carrie smiled wider and nodded her head with delight. The teacher knew her name.

Laura had seen a young man who boarded at the hotel eating supper in the dining room every evening. He was always nicely dressed in a black waistcoat and starched white shirt and black tie. But she had not known he was a teacher. No one had said anything. Of course, she'd been in the hotel only barely more than a week. And all that the Steadam boys wanted to do was make her and her sisters miserable. They would not have mentioned Mr. Reid.

Mr. Reid smiled at Laura.

"You are Laura?" he asked.

Laura nodded.

"And Mary," he said, looking at Mary.

"Good morning, Mr. Reid," said Mary with her best manners.

"Good morning, Mary," answered Mr. Reid.

As the girls moved past the teacher on into the schoolroom, Laura thought, "It will be very strange, making up my teacher's room every Saturday!" On Saturdays the girls helped Ma tend the boarders' rooms.

Laura set her lunch pail on the bench near the water bucket, and she peeked around the cloakroom wall and into the classroom. And there they were, Johnny and Ruben Steadam, sitting together at a desk.

"Oh, no," Laura said to herself.

Her eyes left the two boys and traveled around the rest of the room. It was a very clean room, with modern desks of shining wood, a large blackboard, a real globe, and maps along one wall and tall windows along another. Even more wonderful, Laura could see, was a long shelf full of books! The school in Walnut Grove had never had extra books.

Laura and Mary sat down at the desk where Mr. Reid directed them, and Carrie shyly scooted beside another little girl her age, who had tight black curls and a pretty pink bow. The little girl said something and Carrie giggled. Laura smiled at them both.

Mr. Reid called the class to order, and he led them in a song and a morning prayer. Laura watched Johnny and Ruben and waited to see them start trouble. She had never seen them sit still and be good for even five minutes.

But to Laura's great surprise, both Ruben and the Holy Terror were being nice boys. And the other big boys in the classroom were also being respectful of Mr. Reid. No one smirked or snickered or shifted noisily in their seats. No one threw anything. They actually seemed to be looking forward to school!

Mr. Reid took a moment to introduce Laura, Mary, and Carrie to the rest of the scholars.

Then he said to Laura and her sisters, "I will hear your reading and recitations later this morning, to determine where to place you in our classroom. But for now I must continue Oliver's story."

And having said that, Mr. Reid walked back to his desk and picked up a large book with leather binding. As he did this, Laura could see Johnny, Ruben, the big boys, and all the rest watching him with intense anticipation.

Mr. Reid looked at Laura, then at Mary.

"This is the story *Oliver Twist*," he told them, "written by the great English novelist Charles Dickens. We are on chapter seven. During our dinner break I will summarize for the new scholars what has already occurred in chapters one through six."

Mr. Reid smiled and nodded his head politely toward the three sisters.

Then he cleared his throat, opened the book, and began to read:

"Noah Claypole ran along the streets at his swiftest pace, and paused not once for breath, until he reached the workhouse-gate. Having rested here, for a minute or so, to collect a good burst of sobs and an imposing show of tears and terror, he knocked loudly at the wicket; and presented such a rueful face to the aged pauper

who opened it, that even he, who saw nothing but rueful faces about him at the best of times, started back in astonishment.

"'Why, what's the matter with the boy!' said the old pauper.

"'Mr. Bumble! Mr. Bumble!' cried Noah. . . ."

Laura was amazed. Mr. Reid was beginning the school day with a novel! And the eyes and ears of every scholar in the room were on him.

Laura listened too. As she did, she realized that Mr. Reid was an extraordinary speaker. He made some words delicate, some words strong, and to Laura the sound of Mr. Reid's elocution was nearly as wonderful as Pa's fiddle. Laura's family had always read aloud to each other. But not in the manner of Mr. Reid. He made everything disappear—the potbellied stove, the globe, the maps, the desk, the world itself—simply by the sound of his voice.

Laura was entranced. And for the first time in her life, she loved words. She loved them as much as the sound of the wind in the trees or the birds in the sky.

Laura might not like the old hotel where she had to live with those bullies, the Steadam boys.

But already she knew that she was going to love the old stone schoolhouse in Burr Oak, Iowa.

SPOTS FOR CHRISTMAS

As the days went by, it seemed to Laura that she spent less and less time with Ma and Pa. Running a hotel was hard work, and it was all Ma could do to keep up with the constant cooking and washing and scrubbing and mopping every day all day long. Before, at least the family had two quiet days a week, Wednesdays for sewing and Sundays for reflection. But the hotel did not stop being a hotel on Wednesdays and Sundays, and those days were as full of the same hard work for Ma as the rest of the week.

And not only did the hotel serve travelers. It often served the town as a place for events. Already one wedding luncheon had been held in the dining room. Laura and Mary had helped serve the delicious pans of beef roast, mashed potatoes, baked kidney beans, creamed corn, homemade cottage cheese, and apples cooked with lemons. For dessert a special brick of ice cream with the shape of a lavender bell in the center was brought in and served beside angel-food cake. Laura had never seen such pretty desserts. But though she and Mary worked very hard all afternoon waiting on everyone, neither sister was offered any ice cream or cake.

Laura did not mind working hard for Ma and Pa. But she minded working hard for un-generous strangers.

And oh, how she missed the calm sweet-ness of her family's having its own house! The hotel was always noisy, with guests trooping upstairs and down, the card playing next door, the Steadam boys yelling and Mrs. Steadam yelling louder. Life with Ma and Pa had always been quiet, and Laura was not used to people who raised their voices and slammed doors.

One day she tried to talk to Pa about it. The snow was deep, and he was out in the barn seeing to Jack and the animals. Jack had actually grown to like the barn, for he'd made friends with a little barn cat. Sometimes Laura looked out the window and saw Jack lying beside the barn on a snowdrift, the little cat asleep on his back.

Laura helped Pa move some hay from the manger into Sam's stall.

"Town life sure is different from farm life," Laura said.

"That it is," Pa answered, hoisting a forkful of hay.

"I like farm life better," said Laura.

"I know, flutterbudget," said Pa. "So do I." Pa hadn't called Laura "flutterbudget" in a long time. Not since he'd grieved over Freddie. Hearing it made Laura glad.

"But don't you worry," Pa continued. "Nothing ever stays the same in this life. We'll not always be living in a hotel in an old town."

"Really, Pa?" asked Laura.

Pa stopped his fork and looked at Laura. Then he smiled.

"You've not heard your last wolf singing its lonely song, I promise. But try to be patient while Ma and Pa pay off their debts and get a fresh start."

A fresh start. Laura had always loved the sound of those words. For they had always meant moving west.

Suddenly she felt happy.

"Yes, Pa," she said.

Pa winked, and they went back to work.

It was mid-December now, and Ma and Mrs. Steadam had decorated the hotel parlor with greenery and with some gold and silver bells left by the previous owner. The bells hung across the fireplace mantel and over the organ.

Laura was afraid to look forward to Christmas this year, though, for she thought it would just mean putting more potatoes on more plates. What she really wanted for Christmas was quiet time with Ma and Pa.

What she got instead was the measles.

Three days before Christmas, Laura woke up early, before Mary or Carrie or even Ma or Pa, and she was terribly thirsty. Thirsty and hot. Her body was so hot that her red flannel gown was wet with perspiration and her long hair stuck to her neck. Laura tried to raise up her head. But she was too tired. She put her head back on the pillow and whispered softly into the darkness.

"Ma?"

Laura coughed a little and whispered again.

"Ma?"

Laura coughed harder. Then Ma was beside her.

"What is it, Laura?" asked Ma.

"I'm hot, Ma."

Ma put her hand on Laura's forehead. Ma's hand felt so dry and cool against the heat of Laura's skin.

"You are ill, Laura," whispered Ma. "Let's get you into bed with Pa and me."

Just as Laura was rising up to go to Ma's bed, another voice whispered into the darkness.

"Ma?" It was Carrie. "I'm sick, Ma." Carrie whimpered a little.

"Goodness," said Ma.

"Me too, Ma," came Mary's voice.

"Gracious!" said Ma.

Ma had three little girls sick with the measles.

Pa rose out of bed and helped Ma tend to

them all. He brought in a pan of cool water and soaked one girl's burning forehead after another while Ma made up some horsemint tea to use as a medicinal.

In the light of the kerosene lamp Pa could see the small red marks flaring up on the girls' white skin.

"You are turning into my sweet red strawberries," Pa said. Laura looked at the spots on the inside of her arm.

"Will they go away, Pa?" she asked. Laura had heard of a terrible sickness called smallpox, and it left ugly marks that never went away.

"Sure they will, half-pint," Pa said as he smoothed Carrie's moist hair back from her face. "But these measles will keep you dotty for at least a week." Ma carried in the teapot and a tin cup. She poured a little tea and gave it to Mary.

"Oh, how I hate to miss school," said Mary after she drank down her tea. The warm aroma of mint floated through the air.

Ma poured another little bit and handed the cup to Carrie.

"School is probably where you got the measles," said Ma. Sickness always spread fast through school. At school everyone used the same dipper to drink out of the water bucket, and they all washed up in the same water in the basin.

Carrie whimpered again.

"Ma," she cried.

"I know, dear child, I know," said Ma, stroking Carrie's hot cheek. "It feels bad."

It felt very bad. Not since the fever 'n' ague she'd had in Indian Territory had Laura felt so sick. She and Carrie stayed in the trundle bed, while Mary took the big bed so as to give them all a little breathing space. They were so hot that Pa even opened the window for them, though it was ten degrees outside and snowing.

All day long the girls suffered. Ma had no help serving breakfast or supper, and Laura and Mary both were sorry that they could not help.

"We're sorry we're sick, Ma," said Mary as Ma came in to check on them after supper had been served and the kitchen cleaned and the dishes washed. "We're sorry we can't help."

"No, no," said Ma, smiling kindly at Mary.

"Everything is just fine. You rest now."

The girls did not complain, for resting was all they could do.

The following afternoon, still hot with fever and sleeping fitfully, Laura suddenly felt her pillow snatched away. Her head bounced with a thump against the mattress.

"Ha-ha!" laughed Johnny Steadam. "Look who's sick!" He ran over and pinched Mary's arm.

"Ow!" she cried. Then he ran out of their room and slammed the door.

"That Johnny Steadam!" grumbled Laura as she picked up her pillow off the floor.

"Johnny's a bad boy," Carrie whispered, then coughed.

Laura found out later from Ma that Johnny's brother, Ruben, had the measles, too.

"I hope Johnny gets them," said Laura.

"Me too," said Carrie. Carrie was curled into a tight little ball with her rag doll and sock doll in her hands. Her face was flushed and her eyes were pink.

"Children," Ma scolded. "You must be kind to Johnny."

Laura said nothing more. But secretly she

wished for Johnny to get *double* measles.

When word got around town that the Ingalls children at the hotel all had the measles, many of the mothers in Burr Oak decided to send their young children over to play with the girls. The mothers were not trying to give the girls company. They were trying to make their own children sick. Measles for a child was not usually a very bad disease, and once over, it would not come back again. But if a grown-up caught the disease, he could die. All the good mothers wanted their children to hurry up and catch the measles before they were grown. So they sent them over to play.

Laura did not want to play. She felt hot and tired, and she wanted to be left alone. Mary and Carrie wanted to be left alone too.

But every day three or four Burr Oak children came into their room to play. They played with Laura's rag doll and with Carrie's rag doll. They played with their paper dolls. They looked through their readers. They bounced on their beds.

"Ohhhhhh," Laura groaned, her face in her pillow, as one little three-year-old boy bounced and bounced and bounced.

It would have been a completely unhappy Christmas for Laura and her sisters if not for one thing: Ma told them that Johnny Steadam now had the measles too. And he had them *very badly*. He was even hotter and more spotted than the girls had been.

Ma waited to see if any of her good girls laughed. But not one of them did. They all looked solemnly at Ma, and not one cracked a smile. Satisfied, Ma went back to work.

But as soon as she left, Laura looked at Carrie and Carrie looked at Mary and Mary looked at them both and they laughed and laughed and laughed!

That was their best Christmas present.

SWEET, CLEAN ROOMS

The day somebody burned out his lungs in the saloon, Pa said he had had enough of hotel life. Laura and her sisters heard him talking it over with Ma after they had all washed and crawled into bed.

"What do you mean he 'burned out his lungs,' Charles?" asked Ma in a hushed voice behind the curtains of the four-poster.

"The fellow drank so much whiskey," said Pa, "that he was full of fumes, and when he

113

tried to light a cigar, he breathed in the flame of the match and burned out his lungs."

"Why, I've never heard of such a thing," said Ma.

"Nor I," said Pa. "But it's just added to my worry about living in this place. So I did some asking around today, and I believe I've found us a new home."

Laura's eyes grew wide in the darkness. Carrie gave a little gasp.

"Where, Charles?" asked Ma.

"Yes, where, Pa?" called Carrie.

"Mind your manners, little girl," Pa said loudly. Then he whispered all the news to Ma. The girls would have to wait and see.

For the next few days Laura was so full of anticipation about a new home, she could hardly concentrate on her lessons at school. Mr. Reid was now on chapter fourteen of *Oliver Twist*, and he was also teaching the children elocution. He selected simple poems for the youngest children or fairy tales like "The Wild Swans" for the oldest, and each day he spent ten minutes with each scholar, concentrating together on making the words sound full and rich and flowing. Laura could hardly believe Ruben Steadam was reciting, *"Far, far away, where the swallows are when we have winter, there lived a king who had eleven sons and one daughter, Elisa,"* without complaint!

Laura tried to pay attention to arithmetic and history and spelling and recitations. But it was hard. Would Pa tell her about the new home today? Where would it be? Could Jack come inside and live with them again?

On their walks home after school, Laura and Mary and Carrie tried to guess whether this would be the day for the good news. But every afternoon they found Ma cleaning the hotel rooms and cooking the hotel's supper as usual, and she did not say anything about moving.

Then, one night at bedtime, as Ma combed the sisters' hair and helped Carrie with her nightgown, she said to them, "Tomorrow you won't be going to school, girls. For tomorrow we are moving."

All three girls jumped with delight.

"Oh, good, oh, good!" Mary said, clapping her hands.

"Where, Ma, where?" asked Carrie.

"Are we going west again?" asked Laura.

Ma smiled and gave them a gentle *shush*.

"Your Pa has rented the rooms above Kimball's Grocery for us," she said. "They're very clean. You will like them."

Laura felt a small pang of disappointment. How she was hoping to go west again! But at least they were getting out of the crowded hotel.

"I can't wait to get away from Johnny and Ruben," said Carrie. "They pull my hair."

"It will be nice to have some privacy again," Ma said. "We will all be better for it."

"Will you and Pa still work in the hotel?" asked Mary.

"No," said Ma. "That is the other good news. Pa will be running his own feed mill, grinding the corn and wheat with Sam and David. And I will stay home, as before."

"Oh, good!" said Mary. "Good, good, good!"

Laura was relieved too. Ma would belong to them again, not to the hotel.

"I can't wait, Ma," said Laura.

"Neither can I," said Ma with a smile.

By the afternoon of the next day, the whole family—Ma, Pa, Laura, Mary, Carrie, and even Jack—were sitting in their own parlor in their own sweet, clean rooms above Kimball's Grocery. They hadn't moved very far. In fact, the grocery sat right next door to the hotel saloon. But still they were as happy as if they'd moved all the way to Oregon, for here life was calm and peaceful. It was so peaceful in these rooms that Laura and her family were very quiet for some time. Pa smoked his pipe and patted Jack's head at his feet. Ma knitted, Mary sewed. Laura read a book of poetry Mr. Reid had lent her, and Carrie cut out new dresses for her paper dolls.

All around them were those things that gave them comfort—the little china shepherdess on the wall, the quiet ticking of their old clock, Ma's Bible and the novel *Millbank*, their own crisp curtains at the clear, clean windows, the shiny black stove keeping their own pot of tea warm, and Ma's wonderful rag rugs brightening the good pine floors.

"Bring me my fiddle box, Laura," said Pa all at once.

Laura had not heard such happy words in a long time. She got Pa's fiddle.

She wondered what Pa would play for them. If it was "Yankee Doodle," it might mean Pa was planning to go west again. He loved "Yankee Doodle" when he had pioneer fever.

But Pa surprised her. He didn't play any of the old songs he used to play, like "Oh, Susanna" or "Buffalo Gals" or "Yankee Doodle."

He played a new song, a song as simple and pure as the new rooms they sat in. And he sang:

"Little drops of water,
Little grains of sand,
Make the mighty ocean,
And the pleasant land.

"Little deeds of kindness,
Little words of love,
Help to make earth happy,
Like the heaven above."

Carrie laughed with delight and clapped her small hands.

"I like happy songs, Pa," she said.

"I know, buttercup," said Pa with a twinkling smile. "I know you do."

Laura looked at Pa's eyes, and she could see there was a light inside them, a light she hadn't seen since they'd left Uncle Peter's house in the cold, dark rain.

Maybe kindness and love were bringing back the light in Pa's eyes.

Laura hoped so.

THE FANCY HOUSE

Across the street from Kimball's Grocery
and the Ingallses' new rooms was the
prettiest house Laura had ever seen.
It was big and white and full of windows. On
its front porch were tall white columns and
carved banisters and a mahogany door decorated with a sunflower window. Ma called this
a stained-glass window and said that there
were a lot of them back east where she grew
up. But Laura had not seen a stained-glass

window until now, and she thought it was beautiful. At night the light inside the house shone through the window and made the yellow sunflower glow.

In the spring Ma made acquaintance with the lady of the pretty white house, and it wasn't long before Ma and her three girls were invited for tea.

Ma put on her best dress of black calico trimmed in white lace, while Laura wore her brown-flecked gingham church dress and Mary and Carrie wore their best dresses, too. Ma carefully tied the girls' long braids with new white ribbon from the mercantile, and her own hair she gathered with the lovely tortoiseshell comb she'd received when she married Pa.

"We must put on our best manners," Ma reminded the girls.

The girls said, "Yes, Ma." They were happy to put on their best manners, especially if it meant they were allowed to have tea at the fancy house.

They crossed the street and walked up to the big front door. Laura looked all around her at the enormous terraced lawn with its lush green grass and beds of roses and its ivy-covered stone walls. She looked very carefully at the sunflower on the door. It was made of many thick pieces of yellow and brown and green glass, each piece outlined by a thin gray material.

Ma ran her finger along the gray line bordering a yellow petal.

"This is lead," Ma explained to the girls. "It is melted and applied around each piece of glass. It holds all the pieces together to make a picture."

Laura looked closely. The lead looked like the same lead that Pa's bullets were made of. She hadn't known lead could also make pretty things.

Ma gave a small tap on the door, and soon it was opened by Mrs. Pifer, the lady of the house, and her two grown daughters, who were introduced as Victoria and Isabel. They were very pretty in their cashmere wrappers and ruffled dresses. Laura suddenly felt awkward and plain.

But she did not feel awkward for long, for Mrs. Pifer and her daughters were warm and gracious, and they seemed delighted to have company.

"Would you like to tour the house?" Isabel

asked Laura and Mary and Carrie.

"Oh, yes!" said Mary. They followed her through the house as Victoria and Mrs. Pifer settled into the parlor to chat with Ma.

"Tea very soon, Isabel!" called Mrs. Pifer.

"Yes, Mama," answered Isabel with a smile. Laura already liked Isabel.

The girls were led into the grand entryway, where two beautiful angel statues had been placed, then up a sweeping staircase and down a long carpeted hallway.

"This is the library," said Isabel, pointing to the right as they moved past an open door with a gilded doorknob. "But it isn't very interesting," she said. "Just books. I'll show you the toy room."

Just books! thought Laura as she craned her neck to peer as far as she could into the room as they walked by. *Just books!*

Laura saw books and books and books. They were along every wall, from the floor to the ceiling. Two thick oak rocking chairs sat in the middle of the room beside a round marble-topped table, also spread with books.

Laura continued down the hall as if in a dream. She could not believe that a person might have her own library. Laura imagined herself stealing into that room, in the deep of night, and reading story after story until dawn. It might take her an entire lifetime to read so many books.

If ever someday I build my own house, thought Laura, *it is going to have a library.*

Isabel led them into the toy room, where Carrie squealed with pleasure at the sight of dozens of beautiful dolls. The dolls were very delicate and made of hand-painted porcelain, and each doll came with her own complete wardrobe. Some had little beds of their own,

and some had little chairs and little tables on which miniature cups and dishes were set.

Isabel smiled and said, "Victoria and I are too big for dolls now, but we still like to visit them and see that they have their tea."

Laura and Mary and Carrie looked at each other with wide eyes. They had never seen a room so marvelous!

Isabel showed them more rooms filled with lovely gilded mirrors and velvet hangings at the windows and silver-plated fruit bowls on little round tables. But Laura would have traded everything, every room and every beautiful thing in it, for the library.

Tea with Mrs. Pifer and her daughters was lovely. Beneath a crystal chandelier, the parlor tea table was spread with a rose-covered cloth, and on this was placed a silver tray with a silver teapot and sugar bowl and cream pitcher. Mrs. Pifer had put a flowered porcelain cup and saucer and small silver spoons with mother-of-pearl handles at each setting. In the center of the table stood a three-tiered plate rack filled with delicate sugar cookies and sweet round biscuits and strawberry tarts. Laura didn't want to eat anything. She wanted to save it all forever. But she bit into a soft sweet biscuit anyway.

During tea, Mrs. Pifer mentioned that her husband had died, and Laura was sad to know that Isabel and Victoria had no father anymore. Laura could not imagine life without Pa. Everything would be lonely and still.

When Ma and the girls said their good-byes after tea, Ma said to Mrs. Pifer, "You and your daughters must come by to see us."

And soon after, the Pifers did just that. They sat in the sunny clean rooms above Kimball's Grocery, in their cashmere wrappers and ruffled dresses and silk bonnets, and they stayed on and on. They seemed not to mind at all that nothing the Ingallses had was grand.

In fact, Mrs. Pifer and her daughters visited quite often, and their company genuinely pleased Ma. On leaving one day, Mrs. Pifer said, "Mrs. Ingalls, we hope we don't impose too much. But you have the coziest home, and we just love sitting here in these pretty, cheerful rooms. We are always a little sorry to return to our own dull house."

Ma blushed with pride at Mrs. Pifer's words, and Laura, too, felt proud. She was proud of

Ma, who always did the best with what she had and who always made things beautiful.

Laura decided she would one day not only have a library. She would also make a cheerful, pretty home. Just like Ma's.

FIRE!

One night Laura was shaken out of sleep
by Ma, standing next to the bed. Jack
was with her, whining and pacing.

"Wake up, children, wake up!" said Ma.
"The saloon's on fire!"

Laura and Mary and Carrie jumped out
of bed.

"Get dressed, girls," said Ma, "for we may
have to run outside if our building catches."

The girls quickly pulled on their dresses

and flannel stockings and ran to look out the windows with Ma.

"Where's Pa?" asked Mary.

"He's gone to help fight the fire," said Ma. Laura could hear the shouts and the confusion of many men in the street down below their rooms.

She and her sisters hurried to look out the window of Ma's bedroom toward the saloon next door. Orange and yellow flames were beginning to crackle up the side of the saloon, right beside the stairs leading to their home, and red-hot embers floated through the air toward them.

"Oh, why don't they hurry?" Laura heard Ma say in the front room. She ran with her sisters to join Ma. Jack was there too, his paws on the windowsill, his hair standing straight up.

Right in front of Kimball's Grocery, in the middle of Main Street, stood the town water pump. From their big windows Laura and her family could watch everything happening. A long line of shouting men with buckets was at the pump.

"Oh, *hurry!*" said Ma. The flames of the

fire were throwing a strange orange light all across the men's faces. Laura watched as one man filled a bucket at the pump and ran. Then the next did the same, and the next.

Carrie said, "Ma, I'm scared." She held tight to Ma's hand.

"Now what is the matter down there?" said Ma. "Why aren't those men *moving*? They aren't moving!"

Laura could see the long line of men stuck at a standstill while the same man stayed at the water pump on and on and on when he should already have filled up his bucket and run.

"He isn't *moving*!" cried Ma.

Laura saw that the man at the pump was Mr. Bisbee, the wealthy boarder at the hotel. And though he was pumping and pumping water into his bucket, his white hair and white whiskers all wild, he was still going nowhere.

"*Fire!*" she could see him yelling, and pumping madly. "*Fire! Fire!*"

"*Move*," said Ma, watching him, her voice low and strained.

Suddenly there was a shout—"*Bisbee!*"— and Laura saw Pa come out of the line and pull

Mr. Bisbee away from the pump. Pa filled his own bucket and ran, and the next man did the same, and soon the bucket brigade was moving quickly again. Mr. Bisbee stood to one side and watched them all, his white hair sticking out, the bucket still in his hand.

"Why didn't Mr. Bisbee move, Ma?" asked Laura.

"I do not know," Ma said with a sigh. "Let us just pray that the fire is put out."

Eventually, with bucket after bucket from the long line of men, the fire was gone. Just a sickly smoke lingered, the smell of it drifting into the Ingalls home and causing them to cover their mouths with damp handkerchiefs. Jack sniffed and sneezed again and again.

"Jack needs a hanky too," said Carrie.

Pa finally came back inside, his face red and sweaty and his clothes sooty. He smelled of smoke.

"Ooh, Pa," said Carrie. "You smell a little."

Pa laughed and went to wash his hands in the basin.

"No, buttercup," Pa said, "I smell a *lot*."

Ma poured Pa a cup of cool water, and they waited to hear him tell of fighting the fire.

"Wouldn't you know," said Pa, "some fellow in the saloon passed out from too much to drink, and he knocked a lantern over on a table. Before anybody knew it, the place was afire."

"Did he die, Pa?" asked Mary.

"No, no one died," answered Pa. "It could have been a lot worse than it was."

"Why did Mr. Bisbee hold up the line, Pa?" asked Laura.

"Yes, Charles," said Ma, "the fire burned on while the gentleman stood there."

Pa smiled and shook his head.

"That Bisbee!" he said. "Why, his bucket had no *bottom* in it! The man was standing there pumping with the water just washing over his feet, and he was so crazy with confusion, he didn't even notice!"

"Oh, Charles!" said Ma, shaking her head in disbelief.

"If I hadn't pulled him off," said Pa, "he'd probably still be there, merrily pumping while the town burned away."

Laura thought about Mr. Bisbee's wild white hair and his bottomless bucket and she smiled. Nothing seemed scary anymore, with Pa telling about crazy Mr. Bisbee.

Pa took a long breath and looked at Ma.

"That blasted saloon," he said. "Every man who worked hardest to put out that fire said he would have let it burn, if it wouldn't have taken the rest of the town with it."

Suddenly Jack reared back and let go the biggest, loudest dog sneeze Laura had ever heard.

"And *somebody* agrees!" said Pa. The family looked over at Jack, who was happily wagging, and they all had a good long laugh.

A REAL HOUSE

Though Mr. Bisbee had frustrated Pa with his bottomless bucket, in the long run Mr. Bisbee proved a worthwhile acquaintance, for in early May, because of him, Laura and her family moved into a real house. A lovely redbrick house on the edge of town.

The house was one of Mr. Bisbee's many pieces of property, and it had been empty for some time, so he wanted someone to rent

it and take care of it. He asked Pa.

"Oh, yes, Charles," Ma had said at supper when Pa told her about it.

"Yes! Yes! Yes!" said Mary and Laura and Carrie.

Everyone wanted a real house again.

So they loaded up the wagon, and with Sam and David again in front and Spot at the rear and Jack trotting beneath, they moved from Kimball's Grocery to the little brick house near the edge of an oak woods.

It was a charming house, with an upstairs and downstairs and a cool, shaded porch and a yard decorated with pink roses and white daisies and blue morning glories on the vine.

The house already had nice pine beds in it, and again Ma and Pa had their own room downstairs and the girls had their own room upstairs. Also upstairs was a sunny extra room, which Ma made into a sewing room because of its cheerful light.

Everyone was so glad to be there. Pa didn't miss the office business of the hotel at all, nor the worry of keeping the guests happy and the saloon calm. He went in high spirits with Sam and David to the feed mill each early morning.

And now that school was over, the three girls stayed contentedly home with Ma. It was May now, and everything was coming alive. All around them was the busy hum of bees and bugs, and new, slithery snakes could be seen scooting along the edges of the gardens. Blue-and-white butterflies drank from the sweet blooming flowers, and overhead thick flocks of water birds—geese and plovers and loons and snipes—flew on their long, joyful journeys north.

And once again Laura was happy to have the responsibility for the cow.

Every warm early morning, Laura rose up, and while her sisters helped Ma with the breakfast, she put on her bonnet to lead Spot to pasture for the day.

Silver Creek flowed near Laura's house, and this was where Spot most loved to stay. Laura left her shoes behind, and barefoot, she and the cow and Jack went early to the shady green grasses beside the creek.

The wind was quieter now, in May, and the songs of birds were everywhere. The *chick-a-dee-dee-dee!* of the friendly, black-capped chickadees. The *perchickory!* of the bright-yellow goldfinches swooping down to prickly patches of thistle for their breakfast. Nearer the creek, in the tangled thickets of the currant bushes, Laura heard the *mrowr!* of the catbird.

Woof! barked Jack. Jack always barked at the catbird.

Laura left Spot beside the creek to chew on the soft green grass and white clover. Then, later in the day, she returned to lead Spot home. Jack came again, too.

And in the heat of the late afternoon, it was bliss to Laura to walk beside the elegant wild flags and wade barefoot into the bubbling creek. She could see the fat gray squirrels traveling through the tops of the tall oak trees above her, and below her was the happy silver dance of hundreds of minnows. Jack lapped and lapped at the minnows.

On her way home, leading a contented cow, Laura picked sheep-sorrel blossoms and dandelion leaves to chew, and she gathered clover branches to bring home to Ma, for they always fragranced the house so nicely. Ma had told Laura that if ever she had a dream about clover, it would foretell a happy marriage, a long life, and prosperity. Laura was still waiting for this dream.

Laura and Spot and Jack all returned home together from the creek meadows, back again down dusty State Street and up to the pretty redbrick house that was, for now, theirs. In the front yard small brown wrens bounced along, their tails held high, their throats full of song. The roses all smelled sweet, and the daisies waved a greeting.

Laura left Spot in the barn. Then she

entered through the back door with Jack.

She said, "I feel happy, Ma."

And Ma, who was pulling a warm lemon pie from the oven, smiled at her and said, "So do I, Laura. So do I."

GRACE COMES

O ne sunny morning toward the end of May, after Laura had taken Spot to pasture and the girls had finished all their chores, Ma asked them to run several errands for her. They were to go to the tin shop and pick up a new lantern for Pa, then to the mercantile for a long piece of braid, then to Kimball's Grocery for flour and sugar, then on to the Burr Oak House to give Mr. Bisbee the June rent.

She also gave them an extra penny, for sugar candy.

"Thank you, Ma!" Carrie said happily.

"Thank you, Ma," said Laura and Mary. Laura did not mind having to run errands. She would be outside, she would get sugar candy, *and* she wouldn't have to sew!

"Take your time," said Ma as the three girls went out the door. "It's a pretty day."

Laura and her sisters walked down Lansing Street and on to the storefronts on Main Street. Horses were tied to hitching posts all along the way, their tails busily flicking away flies. Laura had actually grown to like Burr Oak. It would never hold her heart the way the west did, but it was a good little town. North to south Silver Creek ran sparkling through its center, and beautiful tall groves of trees surrounded the town on every side. Beyond, soft rolling fields stretched out to the horizon. Laura liked a new town better, but for an old town, Burr Oak was a fine one.

Laura and Mary and Carrie ran all of Ma's errands. Then they stopped at the Burr Oak House to leave the rent for Mr. Bisbee. They knew better than to carry any candy with

them to the hotel, for Johnny and Ruben
might try to take it. The girls would save
buying their candy for last.

They walked up to the hotel and stepped
inside the parlor. Laura could hear the clang of
pots and Mrs. Steadam's loud talk down in the
kitchen, and Laura was very glad she never had
to sleep in that little room downstairs again.
But she still liked the hotel. It was nice to see
the pretty parlor and the big Bent organ again.

Mr. Steadam and Johnny were in the hotel
office. Johnny had grown taller through the
year—to Laura he seemed almost like one of
the big winter boys at school—but he'd not
grown any nicer. He sneered at the girls.

"Hello, Mr. Steadam," said Mary. "We'd like
to leave our rent here for Mr. Bisbee, if we may."

"Sure, I'll take it," said Mr.
Steadam, reaching for the
money and then turning
toward his safe. That
was all he said. Mr.
Steadam had never
been friendly, like
Pa.

The girls turned

to go. As she followed Mary and Carrie through the door, Laura felt a sudden sting on her neck.

"Ow!" she said. She looked behind her. Johnny Steadam had a big grin on his face and a paper tube in his hand. He'd shot a spitball at her.

Laura stuck out her tongue at him and walked on.

Mary had seen her.

"Laura!" she said. "What would Ma say?"

"She'd say 'Ow!' too," said Laura. Carrie giggled. Mary just sighed.

The girls bought three striped sticks of sugar candy and walked slowly home, waiting a long time between licks to make the candy last. As they neared their house, they saw Jack on the front porch, pacing. Laura could hear his whine.

"Something's the matter," Mary said. They hurried up to the porch, past Jack, and into the house.

Pa was sitting there in the parlor rocker, smoking his pipe, and off in the kitchen Laura could see one of the neighbor women at the stove.

Laura looked at Mary. Then they both looked at Carrie. And this time, because Carrie remembered some things, she looked back at them with a happy face.

Pa smiled at his girls.

"Ma's got a little bundle of surprise for you, girls," he said, his blue eyes twinkling. "Want to see?"

"Oh yes, Pa!" said Laura. With her sisters she followed Pa into Ma's bedroom.

Ma was plumped up in her big bed under the quilts. And in her arms, wrapped in flannels, was a beautiful pink sleeping baby.

Laura and Mary and Carrie shyly stepped nearer.

"Her name is Grace," said Ma. "Grace Pearl." Ma's face was shining, her eyes were shining. Laura thought she glowed happy as the sun.

"She's beautiful, Ma," said Mary.

Carrie bent over and kissed the baby's nose.

"I love her," said Carrie.

Laura couldn't help thinking of little Freddie. She almost felt an ache rise up in her throat. But she didn't let it.

"She's an angel, Ma," Laura said.

Ma looked at Laura, and for a moment Laura thought she saw some of that same ache on Ma's face. But then Ma smiled and she said, "Do you know what 'grace' means?"

The girls all shook their heads.

"It means the spirit of God in someone's heart," said Ma. And her eyes filled with happy tears.

Mrs. Starr

One evening in June, when Laura came home with the cow, Ma and baby Grace did not meet her at the barn, as Ma liked to do. Laura went into the house alone.

There in the parlor with Ma sat Mrs. Starr from town. She was the doctor's wife, and Laura saw her with Dr. Starr every Sunday at the Congregational church. Mrs. Starr was a nice, well-mannered person, and Laura was always happy to greet her at church. But she wondered what Mrs. Starr was doing in the parlor, for she had never visited before.

"Come in, Laura," said Ma when she saw Laura standing in the kitchen.

Laura stepped into the parlor, and she smiled at Mrs. Starr.

"Hello, Mrs. Starr," said Laura.

Mrs. Starr smiled back and held out her arm for Laura to come closer. Laura did, and Mrs. Starr put her arm around Laura's waist and hugged her tenderly.

Then Mrs. Starr said, "Laura dear, I would like you to come home with me and be my own little girl."

Laura felt shy at Mrs. Starr's teasing and looked down at the floor.

"I have been talking everything through with your mother," said Mrs. Starr.

Suddenly, at the sound of Mrs. Starr's voice, Laura realized she wasn't teasing at all. Mrs. Starr was serious.

"My own little girls, Ida and Fay, are all grown up now, and they have gone away to be teachers," Mrs. Starr continued. As she listened to the woman's voice, Laura began to feel strange inside, as if she were floating, as if she were dreaming.

"And I am very lonely with no little girl around the house anymore," said Mrs. Starr. "Your mother and father have four little girls, and that is a lot of little girls to take care of."

Laura's heart was pounding. It didn't seem real, that someone had come to take her away.

Mrs. Starr spoke again to Ma.

"As I was saying, Mrs. Ingalls, Dr. Starr and I will adopt Laura and care for her as if she were our own. She will have everything we gave our own girls: the best education, music lessons, lovely clothes. All she could ever want. And when we pass away, Laura will have a share in our property equal with Ida's and Fay's."

Laura could not believe what she was hearing, and she could not bear to look up from the floor at Ma. She could not risk seeing Ma's face. Would Ma really give her away?

Ma was silent.

Softly Mrs. Starr said, "Please, Mrs. Ingalls. You and your husband are struggling with four children. Let us have Laura."

Laura was ready then to plead with her ma, to plead with her not to give her away. Laura raised her head and looked desperately at Ma's face.

But Ma was smiling at Laura, and her calm eyes told Laura that everything would be all right. Ma had been polite and had kindly listened to Mrs. Starr's offer. But she answered, "I do understand, Mrs. Starr, and I am very sorry, but Charles and I couldn't possibly spare Laura."

Mrs. Starr gave a gentle sigh. Then she loosened her arm from around Laura's waist. She nodded.

"Thank you for your time, Mrs. Ingalls," she said. Then Ma saw her to the door and she went away.

When Ma turned back inside, she looked at Laura with a sympathetic smile.

"She is a sad, lonely woman," said Ma. And that was all that Ma ever said.

But for days afterward an awful feeling stayed with Laura. It was fear, fear that somehow she might have been taken away. And though she would still have been the same girl, with the same face and the same mind, she would not have been Laura Ingalls and she would not have belonged to Ma and Pa and

Mary and Carrie and Grace, and they would have gone on being who they were without her.

Every time Laura thought of this, it made her afraid, and she tried to forget it as quickly as she could.

A PEACEFUL PLACE

Baby Grace was a beautiful, healthy child. At two months she was rosy cheeked and chubby, and her hair was golden like Mary's, her eyes bright blue like Pa's. Grace was never ill, she never even sneezed, and Laura did not worry they might lose her.

All the sisters loved taking care of Grace, and with a cozy little house and the warm yellow days of summer, they could not be more content. Laura even made a new friend. Her name was Alice.

Alice was nearly ten years old, just like Laura, and they had been school friends, but now that school was out, they were summer friends, too. Alice had pretty red hair, which she wore in braids like Laura's, and her mother made her lovely bonnets trimmed in crochet. Laura's bonnets were all plain.

Alice and Laura loved to explore Burr Oak in the afternoons when their chores were done. They always met at the Methodist church, for it was halfway between their houses. Sometimes they arrived at the church at the same time. Other days Laura would find Alice waiting on the steps or Alice would find Laura waiting. They were always happy to see each other.

Some days the two friends walked west of town to the old quarry, and they looked down into the open gorge where men had cut big chunks of stone for building houses. A few times they had walked east, up to the swimming hole near a large shady grove. But Ma didn't like Laura going up there with only Alice, for Laura did not know how to swim and Ma was afraid she might drown. So the girls stopped going there.

They sometimes visited the barn of the Burr Oak House to pet the little cat that used to sleep on Jack's back. The little cat was now a mama cat, for she had given birth to nine kittens, and they all followed her everywhere. Alice and Laura sat in the hayloft and let the kittens crawl up their arms and backs and nuzzle into their necks. Laura wanted very much to take one home.

"I wish I could take the little gray one home," she told Alice one day in the barn.

"I wish I could take the striped one," said Alice.

"But my Pa won't let me," they both said at the *very same time!* They looked at each other in surprise, then laughed and laughed.

But of all the places in Burr Oak to visit, the cemetery was their favorite.

Laura had never seen a real town cemetery before coming to Burr Oak. When she'd first traveled west from the little house in the big woods of Wisconsin, she had seen many grave markers along the trail. Pioneers died of many things—cholera, scarlet fever, diphtheria, typhus—and if they died on the trail, their families had to bury them and leave them behind. Laura had seen many grave markers on her journey west, sometimes one sitting all alone or sometimes two or three together there on the empty plain. Even little Freddie's grave was alone.

So Laura did not know about cemeteries, nor how pretty they could be, until Alice took her to the one at the south end of town one afternoon.

As they walked farther down dusty Main Street and away from the stores, Laura could see up ahead the swaying, graceful branches of many evergreen trees. When she drew nearer the trees, she saw two tall wrought-iron gates latched together, and a wrought-iron sign arching above them that read BURR OAK CEMETERY.

"The gate is usually closed, unless there's a funeral," said Alice. "But we can get in over here." She pointed to a smaller gate farther down, which was left open for people to walk through.

Laura stepped inside the cemetery. It was very quiet, and it made her feel quiet inside. It must have made Alice feel the same way, for neither girl talked much while they were there.

They spent the entire afternoon in the cemetery that first day. The grass was soft and thick—like a green, comforting blanket—and velvety moss grew in little hollows and on the tombstones themselves. The big evergreen trees cast cool, dark shadows here and there, and in the sunnier places sweet williams, white roses, and bright-blue coneflowers swayed in the breeze.

Laura and Alice walked among the tombstones and read the markings aloud:

GWENDOLYN ELLIS
Born Jan 13, 1814
Died Sept 11, 1849
Mother rest in quiet sleep
while friends in sorrow o'er thee weep

RICHARD A. SYMMS
Died May 14, 1864
Aged
51 yrs. 8mo's & 14 days
He died as the good man dieth

LILLIE LOUISE JACKSON
1821–1842
She shall be carried into paradise

Laura felt somehow comforted by these remembrances, and she loved the poetry of the words.

"When I grow old and die," said Alice, "I won't mind lying down in such a peaceful place to wait for Judgment Day."

Laura gazed at all the quiet beauty around her—the tombstones dappled in sunlight and shadow, the lovely flowers, the noble trees—and she thought she wouldn't mind either.

Before the sun went down, the two good friends left the cemetery and walked back through town toward home. Alice's home came first, so Laura said good-bye to her there. Then Laura walked alone.

Back at the little brick house, Ma and Mary were in the kitchen slicing potatoes while beans baked for supper. Carrie was playing with baby Grace on the parlor floor. And Pa was out in the barn with Jack.

"Did you have a nice time with your friend today?" asked Ma when Laura came through the door.

"Yes, Ma," said Laura. "I surely did."

WEST, AT LAST

One morning in September, Ma called Laura and her sisters out of bed.

"Wake up, children," Ma said softly. "Put on your dresses now, for Pa is nearly packed and ready to go."

Laura's eyes flew open in the dim light. She looked up at Ma.

"Am I dreaming, Ma?" Laura asked.

"No, dear," said Ma. "We are going west again and want an early start. Now hurry along, so you can help Pa."

Quickly Laura and Mary and Carrie climbed out of bed and gathered their stockings and petticoats and dresses. Laura was so excited that her heart was pounding. Pa had been talking about the west for days. But he hadn't said anything about moving.

With her sisters Laura ran downstairs into the parlor. It was empty! Only a lantern stood in the corner, shining a dim light on the floor. Pa's wooden bracket and the china shepherdess were gone. Ma's rocker was gone. Everything was gone.

Ma stepped out of the kitchen, carrying Grace. She handed the baby to Mary.

"Mary, tend to Carrie and Grace while I gather the quilts. Laura, you can help Pa outside."

Laura put on her shoes, then stepped out into the yard. Pa had already hitched up Sam and David to the wagon and tied Spot behind. He was lifting up the cookstove now. Jack ran from the front of the wagon to the back, then to the front again, his tail wagging with joy. Jack was a traveling dog.

Laura walked over to Pa. The sun's soft morning light was just beginning to spread along the far edges of the rolling land around her.

"Are we really going west again, Pa?" Laura asked.

Pa settled the stove in its place, then turned to look at her. He was smiling.

"The west is calling our name, flutter-budget," Pa said. "I told you nothing ever stays the same."

Laura smiled back at him. It was really true.

Pa helped Laura and her sisters into the wagon bed. It was already packed tight with the barrels of flour and cornmeal and the sacks of beans and rice and all their other food. The box of dishes and the boxes of clothes were packed. The stove and the straw-tick mattress were in. And safe inside a warm little box of woolen blankets they settled baby Grace.

Pa climbed onto the wagon seat beside Ma, and he flicked the horses' reins. The wagon rolled away. It rolled away from the little brick house where Grace was born. It rolled away from the sweet, clean rooms above Kimball's Grocery. It rolled away from the Burr Oak House.

Laura sat in the back of the wagon, looking

out into the gentle light toward the old town they were leaving behind.

"Good-bye, Alice," she called in her thoughts. "Good-bye, Mr. Reid. Good-bye, everybody."

Laura suddenly felt a hurt in her throat, which meant she wanted to cry. But she would not cry.

For Laura wanted more than anything to go west again. She wanted to go back to the tall-grass prairie. She wanted to go back to the enormous sky. She missed the emptiness.

Laura couldn't wait for a fresh start.